GHOST
KNIGHT

GHOST KNIGHT

CORNELIA FUNKE

TRANSLATED BY OLIVER LATSCH

Little, Brown and Company
New York Boston

Text copyright © 2011 by Cornelia Funke
Illustrations copyright © 2012 by Andrea Offermann
English translation copyright © 2012 by Oliver Latsch

Little, Brown and Company

Hachette Book Group
237 Park Avenue, New York, NY 10017
Visit our website at www.lb-kids.com

Little, Brown and Company is a division of Hachette Book Group, Inc.
The Little, Brown name and logo are trademarks of Hachette Book Group, Inc.

The publisher is not responsible for websites (or their content) that are not owned by the publisher.

First U.S. Paperback Edition: May 2013
First U.S. hardcover edition published in May 2012 by Little, Brown and Company
Originally published as *Geister Ritter* in Germany by Cecilie Dressler Verlag in August 2011

Library of Congress Cataloging-in-Publication Data

Funke, Cornelia Caroline.
[Geister Ritter. English.]
Ghost knight / Cornelia Funke ; [illustrations by Andrea Offermann] ; translated by Oliver Latsch. — 1st ed.
p. cm.
Summary: Eleven-year-old Jon Whitcroft and new friend Ella summon the ghost of Sir William Longspee, who may be able to protect Jon from a group of ghosts that threatens him harm from the day he arrives at Salisbury Cathedral's boarding school. Includes historical notes.
ISBN 978-0-316-05614-4 (hc) / 978-0-316-05616-8 (pb)
[1. Ghosts—Fiction. 2. Knights and knighthood—Fiction. 3. Boarding schools—Fiction.
4. Schools—Fiction. 5. Friendship—Fiction. 6. Salisbury Cathedral—Fiction.
7. Salisbury (England)—Fiction. 8. England—Fiction.] I. Offermann, Andrea, ill.
II. Latsch, Oliver. III. Title.
PZ7.F96624Gfm 2012
[Fic]—dc23   2011025420

10 9 8 7 6 5 4 3 2 1

RRD-C

Book design by Alison Impey

Printed in the United States of America

*For Ella Wigram, who was my inspiration
for the heroine in this story.*

I couldn't have invented a better one.

DEPORTED

I was eleven when my mother sent me to boarding school in Salisbury. Yes, granted, she did have tears in her eyes as she brought me to the station. But she still put me on that train.

"Your father would have been so happy about you going to his old school!" she said, forcing a smile onto her lips. And The Beard gave me such an encouraging slap on the shoulder that I nearly shoved him onto the rails for it.

The Beard. The first time my mother brought him home, my sisters immediately crawled onto his lap. I, however, declared war on him as soon as he put his arm around Mum's shoulder. My father had died when I was four, and of course I missed him, even if I barely remembered him. But that *definitely* did not mean I wanted a new father, especially not one in the shape of an unshaven dentist. I was the man around the house, uncontested hero to my sisters and apple of my mother's eye. Suddenly she no longer watched television with me in the evenings but instead went out with The Beard. Our dog, who would chase anyone off our grounds, put squeaky toys in front of The Beard's feet, and my sisters drew oversize hearts for him. "But he's so nice, Jon!" I heard over and over. *Nice.* And what exactly was so nice about him? That he convinced my mother everything I liked to eat was bad for me? Or that he told her I watched too much TV?

I tried every trick in the book to get rid of him. At least a dozen times I disappeared the house keys Mum had given him. I poured Coke over his dentistry magazines (yes, there are magazines for dentists). I mixed itching powder in his beloved mouthwash. All useless. In the end it wasn't him but me whom Mum put on the train. *Never underestimate your enemies!* Longspee would teach me that later. But I hadn't met him yet.

My banishment had probably been decided after I convinced my youngest sister to pour her oatmeal into his shoes. Or maybe it was the WANTED TERRORIST poster into which I'd Photoshopped his picture. Whatever it was, I'd bet my game console that the boarding school was The Beard's idea, even though my mother denies it to this day.

Of course Mum offered to deliver me personally to my new school and to stay for a few days in Salisbury "until you find your feet." But I refused. I was positive she just wanted to soothe her guilty conscience because she was planning to go on to Spain with The Beard while I, on my own, would have to deal with totally new teachers, bad boarding-school food, and new classmates, most of whom were probably going to be stronger and way smarter than me. I'd never spent more than a weekend away from my family. I didn't like sleeping in strange beds, and I definitely didn't want to go to school in a town that was more than a thousand years old—and even proud of it. My eight-year-old sister would have loved to swap with me. She'd been reading *Harry Potter*, and she was desperate to go to a boarding school. I, however, had nightmares of children in hideous uniforms, sitting in dingy halls in front of bowls filled with watery porridge, watched by teachers with yardsticks.

I didn't speak a word all the way to the station. I didn't even give my mother a kiss good-bye after she had hoisted my suitcase onto the train. I was too afraid I'd collapse into a sobbing, childish mess in front of The Beard. I spent the entire train ride cutting and gluing ransom notes from old newspapers, threatening The Beard with all manner of terrible, painful deaths if he didn't leave my mother immediately. The old man sitting next to me kept looking over with increasing alarm, but in the end I threw the letters away in the train's lavatory. I told myself that my mother would probably figure out who'd composed those letters and that she would just end up preferring The Beard over me even more.

I know. I was in a pathetic state. The train ride lasted for one hour and nine minutes. That's now more than eight years ago, and I still remember it perfectly. Bristol — Bath — Westbury. The train stations all looked the same, and with every passing mile I felt more banished. After half an hour I had devoured all the chocolate bars Mum had packed for me (nine, as I remember — she'd felt really guilty!). Every time I looked out the window and everything started looking blurry, I told myself it wasn't tears but the rain running down the windowpane that distorted my vision.

As I said, pathetic.

While I was dragging my suitcase out of the train in Salisbury, I felt terribly young and at the same time aged by a hundred years. Banished. Homeless. Mother-, dog-, and sisterless. A curse on The Beard! I dropped the suitcase on my foot, sending a prayer to hell, begging for some contagious disease that affected only dentists vacationing in Spain.

Anger felt much better than self-pity. Also, it was useful armor against all the curious looks.

"Jon Whitcroft?"

In contrast to The Beard, the man who was taking the suitcase out of my hand and shaking my chocolate-covered fingers didn't have even the shadow of a beard. Edward Popplewell's round

face was as hairless as mine (and caused him much distress, as I was soon to find out). His wife's upper lip, however, was sprouting a dark mustache. Alma Popplewell's voice was also deeper than her husband's.

"Welcome to Salisbury, Jon!" she said, suppressing a little shudder as she pressed a handkerchief into my sticky fingers. "You can call me Alma, and this is Edward. We are the house wardens. Your mother told you we'd be picking you up, didn't she?"

She smelled so intensely of lavender soap that I nearly gagged—or maybe it was the chocolate bars. Wardens…great! I wanted my old life back: my dog, my mother, my sisters (though I could have done without them), and my friends at my old school…no Beard, no beardless warden, and no lavender-soapy housemother.

The Popplewells were, of course, used to homesick newbies. As we left the station, Edward the Beardless placed his hand firmly on my shoulder, as if wanting to squash any thoughts of escape. The Popplewells didn't drive. (There were some nasty rumors that this was due to Edward's great love of whiskey and his firm belief that its regular consumption might yet sprout some stubble on his baby-smooth cheeks.) Whatever the reason, we went on foot, and Edward began to tell me as many facts about Salisbury as could be crammed into a thirty-minute walk. Alma interrupted her husband only when he mentioned dates, for those he confused quite often. But she might as well not have bothered. I wasn't really listening anyway.

Salisbury. Founded in the damp mists of prehistory. Fifty thousand inhabitants and more than three million tourists who come every year to stare at its cathedral. The town welcomed me with pouring rain. The cathedral stuck its tower out from among the wet roofs of the city like a warning finger. *Hear ye, Jon Whitcroft and all sons of his world. Thou art fools for believing your mothers love you more than anyone else.*

I looked neither left nor right as we walked down a

street that had already been there when the Black Death had last come through town. Somewhere along the way Edward Popplewell bought me an ice cream ("Ice cream tastes nice even in the rain, am I right, Jon?"), but in my world-weariness I didn't even manage to squeeze out a "thank you." Instead, I imagined spreading chocolate stains over his pale gray tie.

It was late September, and despite the rain the streets were packed with tourists. The restaurants were all offering fish-and-chips specials, and the window of a chocolate shop actually did look quite alluring, but the Popplewells steered straight toward the gate in the old city wall, which is flanked by little shops, all offering cathedrals, knights, and water-spitting demons cast in silvery plastic. It was the vista beyond the gate that had all the strangers with their garish backpacks and packed lunches filing down Main Street. I didn't even lift my head as the Cathedral Close opened up in front of me. I didn't give a glance to the cathedral and its rain-darkened tower, nor to the old houses that surround it like a clutch of well-dressed servants. All I saw

was The Beard, sitting on our couch in front of our television, my mother to his right, my sisters to his left, fighting over who got to climb into his lap first, and Larry, the treacherous dog, rolled up by his feet. While the Popplewells were exchanging words above my head, arguing over the exact year in which the cathedral had been completed, I saw my deserted room and my deserted chair in my old classroom. Not that I'd ever particularly enjoyed sitting on it, but suddenly the thought of it nearly brought me to tears — which I quickly wiped away with Alma's lavender-reeking (and now chocolate-brown) handkerchief.

Most of the memories of the day of my arrival are shrouded in thick mists of homesickness. Though if I try really hard, I can make out some blurry images: the gate of the old boardinghouse ("Built in 1565, Jon!" "Nonsense, Edward, 1685!"), narrow corridors, rooms that smelled of alienness, strange voices, strange faces, food that was so tainted with homesickness that I barely managed to keep even a few bites down....

The Popplewells put me in a three-bed room.

"Jon, these are Angus Mulroney and Stuart Crenshaw," Alma announced as she pushed me into the room. "You'll soon be best friends, I'm sure."

Really? And what if not? I thought as I eyed the posters my new roommates had plastered all over the walls. Of course, there was one of that band I particularly hated. At home I'd had my own room, with a sign on the door: STRICTLY NO ADMISSION TO STRANGERS AND FAMILY MEMBERS. There, nobody had snored next to me or underneath me; there had been no sweaty socks on the carpet (except my own), no music I didn't like, no posters of bands *and* football teams I despised. At that point my hatred for The Beard reached a level that would have been a credit even to Hamlet. (Not that I knew anything about Hamlet back then.)

Stu and Angus tried their best to cheer me up, but I was too despondent to even remember their names at first. I didn't take any of the gummy bears they offered me from their top secret (and highly illicit) stash of sweets. When my mother called that evening, I left her in little doubt that she had sacrificed the happiness of her only son for that of a bearded stranger, and when I hung up, it was with the grim knowledge that she was going to be spending as sleepless a night as I.

Boarding school. Lights out at eight thirty. Luckily, I'd thought to pack my flashlight. I spent hours drawing gravestones with The Beard's name on them, all the time cursing the hard mattress and the stupidly flat pillow.

Yes, my first night in Salisbury was pretty grim. The reasons for my deep sadness were, of course, pathetic compared to what was yet to come. But how could I have known that homesickness and The Beard would soon be the least of my problems? Since that time I have often asked myself whether there is such a thing as fate, and if there is, whether there's a way to avoid it. Would I have ended up in Salisbury even if my mother hadn't fallen in love again? Or would I never have met Longspee, Stourton, and Ella if it hadn't been for The Beard? Maybe.

THREE DEAD MEN

The next day I got to see my new school. It was only a quick walk from the boardinghouse across the Cathedral Close, and this time I at least gave the cathedral a sleepy glance as Alma Popplewell led me past it. The street behind it is lined with oak trees, and it resounded with the screams of terrifyingly awake first graders. Alma put a protective arm around my shoulder, which was quite embarrassing, especially when a group of girls walked past us.

The school grounds are at the end of the street, behind a wrought-iron gate that could easily tear your trousers when you climbed over it. On that morning, however, it was wide open. The crest on the gate shows just one disappointing white lily on blue ground. No dragons, or unicorns, or lions, like on the crest above the gate to the city.

"Well, this is, after all, also the royal crest of the Stuarts, Mr. Whitcroft!" Mr. Rifkin, my new history teacher observed drily after I complained about it a few days later. He then launched into a torturous hour of explaining how exciting heraldic animals would be entirely inappropriate for a cathedral school.

While my old school had resembled a

concrete box, the new one was a palace. "Erected in 1225, as the bishop's official residence," Alma explained in a raised voice as she navigated us through a throng of noisy and disconcertingly large boys.

I was sick with fear, and I got very little comfort from picturing how I would hang The Beard from one of the huge trees that stand on the school's lawn.

Alma continued her lecture while we crunched across the gravel toward the entrance. "The main building was erected in 1225. In the fifteenth century, Bishop Beauchamp had the east tower added. The facade is…" And so on and so forth. She even recited the names of countless bishops who had resided there. One of my new schoolmates later let me in on the secret that pelting the foreheads of the episcopal portraits that line the staircase is supposed to bring good luck on tests. It never worked for me, though. Anyway...of all the information Alma crammed into my weary head on that first morning, the only fact I recall is that behind one of the many windows James II got a nosebleed—so bad that he stayed in bed for days instead of facing William of Orange on the battlefield.

I didn't learn much else on that first school day. I was far too busy trying to remember names and faces and not to get lost in the labyrinth of corridors and staircases. I had to face the facts that my schoolmates did not look starved and that I wouldn't find any of those dark halls I'd seen in my nightmares. Even the teachers were bearable. However, none of that changed that I'd been banished, and so I returned to Angus and Stu in the evening with the same gloomy face I'd put on that morning in front of the bathroom mirror. I was the Count of Monte Cristo, who would one day return from the terrible prison island to take revenge on all those who had sent him there. I was Napoléon, banished to die a lonely death on Saint Helena. I was Harry, locked up under the Dursleys' staircase.

The house in which I spent the dark nights of my banishment could not claim any stories about royal nosebleeds, even though it was also quite old. Its interior, however, had long been taken over by the twenty-first century: linoleum floors, bunk beds, washrooms, and a television room on the ground floor. The girls had the first floor; the boys lived on the second.

In our room, Angus was the uncontested inhabitant of the single bed. Angus was taller than I by at least a head; he was three-quarters Scottish (and never talked about the other quarter) and quite a good rugby player. And he was one of the Chosen, as we less fortunate ones called the choristers. They wore robes that were nearly as old as the Bishop's Palace, they got excused from class to attend rehearsals, and they sang not only in the cathedral but also in such exotic places as Moscow and New York. (I was not surprised when I wasn't picked at the auditions, but Mum was crushed. After all, my father had been a chorister.)

The wall over Angus's bed sported photographs of his dog, his two canaries, and his tame turtle, but none of the human members of his family. When Stu and I finally got to meet them, we quickly realized that they actually didn't look half as nice as the dog and the canaries, though Angus's grandfather did bear some resemblance to the turtle. Angus slept under a mountain of fluffy toys, and he wore pajamas with dogs printed on them. I quickly found out that both of those facts were best left unmentioned, unless you were keen to learn firsthand what a "Scottish Hug" felt like.

Stu occupied the top bunk, leaving me the bottom one, with his mattress looming above. During the first nights the creaks and groans of Stu turning above kept yanking me out of my sleep. Stu was only marginally taller than a squirrel, and he had so many freckles that all of them barely fit on his face. And Stu was such a windbag that I quickly learned to appreciate the moments when Angus would just hold Stu's mouth shut. Stu's passions included neither stuffed toys nor doggyprint pajamas. He loved covering his scrawny body with fake tattoos, which he painted with permanent markers on every accessible bit of skin — although Alma Popplewell would mercilessly scrub them off at least twice every week.

The two of them did their level best to try to cheer me up, but making new friends just didn't fit with my status of being banished and miserable. Luckily, neither Angus nor Stu took my gloomy silence personally. Angus himself still suffered bouts of homesickness, even though he was already in his second year of boarding there. And Stu was far too preoccupied with falling in love with every halfway-acceptable female at the school.

It was on my sixth night that I realized homesickness was going to be the least of my worries. Angus was humming in his sleep, some tune he was practicing for the choir. I lay awake, wondering once again who would be the first to give in: my mother, because she'd finally realize that her only son was far more important than a bearded dentist, or me, because I'd get tired of my leaden heart and beg her to let me come home.

I was just about to pull the pillow over my head to block out Angus's sleepy singsong, when I heard horses

snorting. I remember wondering, as I tiptoed toward the window, whether Edward Popplewell had taken to traveling to the pub on horseback. Angus's humming, our clothes all over the floor, the cheesy nightlight Stu had put on the desk — none of those things could possibly have prepared me for seeing something scary in the soggy night outside.

But there they were.

Three riders. Very pale. As if the night air had gone moldy. And they were staring up at me.

Everything about them was drained of color: capes, boots, gloves, belts — and the swords hanging from their sides. They looked like men who'd had their blood sucked out by the night. The tallest one's straggly hair hung down to his shoulders, and I could see the bricks of the garden wall through his body. The one next to him had a hamster face and, just like the third ghost, was so see-through that the tree behind him seemed to grow right through his chest. Their necks were marked with dark bruises, as if someone had tried to slice their heads off with a very blunt knife. But the most horrible thing about them was their eyes: burned-out holes filled with bloodlust. To this day those eyes scorch holes into my heart.

Their horses were as pale as the riders. Ashen fur hung from the animals' skeletal bodies like tattered rags.

I wanted to cover my eyes so I wouldn't have to see the bloodless faces anymore, but I was so scared that I couldn't even lift my arms.

"Hey, Jon, what are you staring at out there?"

I hadn't even heard Stu climb out of his bunk.

The tallest ghost pointed a bony finger at me, and his shriveled lips mouthed a silent threat. I stumbled back, and Stu pushed in next to me and pressed his nose against the windowpane.

"Nothing!" he observed disappointedly. "I can't see anything."

"Leave him alone, Stu!" Angus muttered sleepily. "He's probably sleepwalking. Sleepwalkers go bonkers when you talk to them."

"Sleepwalking? Are you blind?" In my panic I talked

so loudly that Stu shot a worried glance toward the door. Luckily, the Popplewells were sound sleepers.

The ghost with the hamster face grinned at me. His mouth was a gaping slit in his pale face. Then he drew his sword, slowly, very slowly. Blood started dripping from the blade, and I felt a pain in my chest so sharp it made me gasp for breath. I fell to my knees and crouched, shivering, under the windowsill.

I can still feel that fear. And I always will.

"Jon! Go back to sleep!" Stu shuffled back toward the bed. "There's nothing out there, 'cept for a bunch of rubbish bins."

He really couldn't see them.

I plucked up all my courage and peered over the windowsill.

The night was dark—and empty. The pain in my chest had gone, and I felt like an idiot.

Great, Jon, I thought as I crawled back under the scratchy blankets. *Now you're officially going crazy.* Maybe it was all a hallucination because I'd barely eaten anything except Stu's gummy bears.

Angus started humming again. I got up a few more times and crept back to the window, but all I saw out there was the deserted street in front of the floodlit cathedral. Finally I managed to fall asleep, having made myself a solemn promise to try to force down at least some of the school's food from then on.

HARTGILL

The next morning I was so tired that I barely managed to tie my shoes. Angus and Stu exchanged a worried look as I went to the window to stare down at the wall where I had seen the ghosts. Yet none of us said a word about what had happened during the night. At breakfast I ate as much oatmeal as I could without throwing up, and then I decided to forget about the whole thing.

By lunchtime I was already back to thinking about

The Beard roasting in the Spanish sun with my mum, and by the afternoon a grammar test had made me forget the three pale figures completely.

It was just beginning to get dark when Mr. Rifkin, as he did every evening, gathered the boarders in front of the school to guide us across the sparsely lit Cathedral Close and back into the care of Alma and Edward Popplewell. None of us liked Rifkin. I believe he didn't even really like himself. He wasn't much taller than any of us, and he would always eye us with a sour face, as if we were causing him a permanent toothache. The only thing that made Mr. Rifkin happy was old wars. He'd enthusiastically grind through at least a dozen sticks of chalk as he sketched on the blackboard the deployment of troops in some famous military encounter or the other. That, as well as his vain attempts to comb his sparse hair over his bald skull, had earned him the nickname Bonapart. (Yes, I know there's an *e* missing — French spelling was not our thing.)

On the lawn in front of the cathedral, the floodlights were just coming on. They bleached the walls, as if someone had rinsed them with moonlight. At that time of evening, the Cathedral Close was nearly empty, and Bonapart impatiently herded us past the rows of parked cars. The air was cool, and while we were all shivering in the damp breeze of an English evening, I wondered whether The Beard had already gotten sunburned and whether that would make him less attractive to my mother.

The three riders were by then no more than a bad dream, washed from memory by the light of day. They had not forgotten about me, however. And this time they made it very clear that they were more than figments of my overactive imagination.

The school's boardinghouse does not stand right on the street. It lies at the end of a broad footpath that branches off the road and leads past a couple of houses toward a gate, beyond which lie the house and its garden. And it was next to that gate that they were waiting for me. They were sitting on their horses, just as they had the night before. Only this time there were four of them.

I stopped so abruptly that Stu stumbled into my back.

Of course, he couldn't see them. Nobody saw them. Except me.

The fourth ghost made the other three look like homeless thugs. His gaunt face was stiff with pompous pride, and his clothes clearly had once been those of a rich man. Yet he also wore iron chains around his wrists and a noose around his neck.

He was so horrible to look at that all I could do was stare at him. Bonapart, however, didn't even turn his head as he walked right past the specter.

As I stood there, unable to move a limb, I heard a whisper inside my head: *Go on, Jon Whitcroft, you might as well face it. Why do you think nobody else can see them? They are after you, and only you!*

But why? I screamed back in my head. *Why me? What do they want from me?*

A raven cawed on a nearby roof, and the ghost leader spurred his horse, as if the bird's hoarse cry had given him a signal. The horse reared with a hollow whinny, and I turned and ran.

I'm not a good runner. That night, however, I was running for my life. Thinking back, I can still feel my heart racing and the searing pain in my lungs. I ran past the old houses that stand in the shadow of the cathedral as if they seek protection from the clamoring world outside the walls; I ran past parked cars, lit windows, and locked gates. *Run, Jon!* Behind me hoofbeats rang out across the darkening close, and I thought I could feel the demonic horses breathing down my neck.

"Whitcroft!" Bonapart screamed my name. "Whitcroft, what the devil is going on? Stop immediately!" But it was the devil who was after me, and then I suddenly heard another voice...if that's what you could call it.

I heard it in my head and my heart. Hollow, hoarse, and so savage that it felt like a blunt knife being driven right through me.

"Yes! Run, Hartgill!" the voice taunted me. "Run! We love nothing better than hunting down your filthy brood. And none of you have evaded us yet."

Hartgill? That was my mother's maiden name. Not

that they looked as if they'd care about such details. I stumbled on, sobbing with terror. The tall one with the straggly hair was cutting me off, and the other three were right behind me. To my right was the cathedral, its tower reaching toward the stars.

Maybe I ran toward it because it looked as if nothing would ever penetrate its walls. The wide lawn that surrounds it was wet from the rain, and I slipped with every step, until I finally ended up on my knees, gasping for air. I curled up on the cold ground, shivering, wrapping my arms over my head as if that could make me invisible to my pursuers. An icy cold enveloped me like a fog. I heard a horse neighing above me.

"A kill without a hunt is only half the sport, Hartgill!" the voice whispered in my head. "Though the hare always ends up dead."

"My...my name is...Whitcroft!" I stammered. "Whitcroft!" I wanted to strike out and kick, send those white corpses back to hell, or wherever they'd come from. Instead, I crouched on the wet grass and nearly threw up.

"Whitcroft!" Bonapart was leaning over me. "Whitcroft, get up!"

Never had I been happier to hear a teacher's voice. I buried my face in the grass and sobbed—this time with relief.

"Jon Whitcroft! Look at me."

I did as Bonapart told me. He looked at my tear-streaked face and quickly fished a handkerchief from his pocket. I reached for it with trembling fingers before carefully peering past him.

The ghosts had gone. As had the voice. But the fear was still there, sticking to my heart like soot.

"Heavens! Whitcroft! Get yourself on your feet already!" Bonapart pulled me up. The other kids were standing by the edge of the lawn, their wide eyes staring at us.

"I can only pray you have an explanation for this pointless sprint through the night?" Bonapart asked, eyeing my muddy pants with obvious disgust. "Or were you trying to prove how fast you can run?"

Puffed-up bastard.

My knees were still shaking, but I tried my best to sound reasonable as I answered him. "There were four ghosts. Four ghosts on horses. They...they were after me."

The whole thing sounded idiotic, even to my ears. I was so embarrassed, I wished the damp lawn would swallow me up on the spot. Fear and shame. Could it get any worse? *Oh, yes, Jon.* It could — and it would.

Bonapart sighed. He glanced at the cathedral with a look of deep exasperation, as if it had been the old church itself that had suggested the story to me.

"Fine, Whitcroft," he said, pulling me rather roughly back toward the street. "It seems to me you've had an unusually intense bout of homesickness. Maybe those *ghosts* ordered you to run right home. Did they?"

We had reached the others again, and one of the girls started giggling. The rest, however, all gave me worried looks, just as Stu had the night before.

I should have bitten my tongue, swallowed my rage over so much blindness and unfair mockery. But I've never been very good at swallowing — still haven't learned it.

"They were there! I swear! How is it my fault that nobody else can see them? They nearly killed me!"

A leaden silence descended on the group. Some of the younger kids inched away from me, as if my madness might be contagious.

"Very impressive!" said Bonapart, his stubby fingers clamped firmly on my shoulder. "I hope you'll show as much imagination in your next history test."

Bonapart only let go of my shoulder when he'd delivered me to the Popplewells. Luckily, he didn't say a word to them about what had happened. Stu and Angus were very quiet during the rest of the evening. By then they were convinced they were sharing their room with a madman, and they were beginning to worry about what was going happen once I completely lost my mind.

Ella

That night, despite everything, Angus and Stu slept soundly, whereas I of course couldn't sleep a wink. In my desperation I even thought about calling my mother. But what was I going to tell her? *Mum, forget about Spain. Four ghosts are hunting me, and their leader called me Hartgill and threatened to kill me?* No. She would tell everything to The Beard, and there was probably not a single dentist on this planet who believed in ghosts. He would just convince her that this was another one of my ploys to make her life difficult.

Get used to it, Jon Whitcroft, I told myself. *Looks like you're not going to be alive to see your twelfth birthday.* And while the sun rose I was wondering whether, after they killed me, I would also turn into a ghost, haunting Salisbury until the end of time, scaring Bonapart and the Popplewells. *It's quite likely, Jon,* I told myself, *but first you have to make sure of one thing: that you don't become the joke of the whole school.* Not that it should have really mattered to someone who was going to be dead soon, but I've never been good at being laughed at.

The next morning I told Angus and Stu that I'd only made up that whole ghost story to fool Bonapart. Both looked at me with great relief (after all, who likes to share a room with a lunatic?), and Stu's concern immediately turned into admiration. During breakfast he spread around my new version of events so successfully that, later, while Bonapart was trying to explain Richard the Lionheart's strategy during the attack on

Jerusalem, two fourth graders started screaming, claiming that they could see his royal ghost, covered in blood, standing by the blackboard. For that they got to join me for detention in the library. At least I was no longer considered crazy but actually some sort of a hero.

If only I could have felt like one. Instead, my fear nearly choked me. During lunch, while all the others were gorging themselves on meat loaf and mashed potatoes, I stared out of the window, wondering whether this gray September day was going to be my last.

I tried to force down a bit of meat loaf, telling myself that I wouldn't be able to run if I starved myself. Suddenly a girl sat down opposite me.

The meat nearly went down the wrong pipe.

That just did not happen. Ever. Girls my age usually stayed well clear of boys. Even the younger girls constantly felt the need to show us older boys how childish they thought we were.

She wasn't one of the boarders, but I had seen her a few times around the school. Her most striking feature was her long dark hair. It fluttered around her like a veil whenever she walked.

"So, there were four?" she said casually, as if asking me about the food on my plate (and there really wasn't much to talk about there).

She eyed me intently, as though she were measuring me inside and out. Only Ella can look at someone like that. But I didn't know her name yet back then. She hadn't introduced herself. Ella never wastes time with unnecessary words.

Despite having two sisters, I wasn't very good at dealing with girls. My sisters may have actually made that worse. I just didn't know what to talk to them about. And on top of that, Ella was pretty—something that would bring an embarrassingly red blush to my face. (Luckily, that's under control now.) So, anyhow, I began to recite my Bonapart prank story. But one cool glance from her made the words die right there on my lips.

She leaned over the table. "Keep that version for the others," she said in a low voice. "What did they look like?"

She wanted to hear the truth. I couldn't believe it. But no matter how much I wanted to talk to someone about it, she was a girl! What if she laughed at me? What if she told all her girlfriends that Jon Whitcroft was an imbecile who actually believed in ghosts?

"They looked dead. How else would they look?" I avoided looking at her by staring down at my fingernails — only to notice that they were dirty. (The presence of a girl makes you notice things like that.) Why the heck wasn't she embarrassed? I gave myself the answer: *Because her kind doesn't get embarrassed like you, you idiot. They also don't start stammering as if they'd forgotten how to talk.*

"What were they wearing?"

Well, if that wasn't a typical girl-question. Ella took my fork and began to eat my mashed potatoes.

"Old-fashioned stuff," I muttered. "Boots, swords..."

"What century?" Ella took another forkful of potatoes.

"What *century?*" I was flabbergasted. "How would I know? They looked like they climbed out of some damn painting." (*Stop cursing, Jon!* I started swearing whenever I became self-conscious. My mother had tried for years to get me to stop.)

"Could you see through them?"

"Yes!" It felt so good to finally talk to someone about the ghosts. Even though I was still struggling with the fact that it was a girl I was talking to.

Ella took in my description as coolly as if I'd been describing our school uniform. "And?" she asked. "Anything else?"

I looked around, but nobody was paying attention to us. "They had bruises on their necks," I whispered across the table. "As if... as if they'd all been hanged. Their leader still has the noose around his neck. And they want to kill me. I know it. They said so."

I admit I expected that piece of information to impress her. But Ella just raised her eyebrows a little. They were very dark eyebrows. Darker than dark chocolate.

"That's nonsense," she observed drily. "Ghosts can't kill anyone. They just can't."

This time I blushed with anger, which wasn't any less embarrassing.

"Well that's great, then!" I hissed at her. "I'll let them know the next time they chase me across the close."

A few third graders at the neighboring table turned toward us. I shot them what I hoped was an intimidating look. I lowered my voice again. "And why," I breathed, while Ella, still perfectly calm, helped herself to another forkful of my potatoes, "did one of them have blood dripping from his sword when I saw them the first time?"

Ella made an unimpressed shrug. "They like doing that sort of thing," she said in a perfectly bored voice. "Blood...bones...it means nothing."

"Oh? Thanks for the insight!" I barked at her. "You seem to know everything about the blasted ghosts in this town. But where I come from it's not at all normal to see them outside your window, pointing bloody swords at you!"

Now the whole dining hall was staring at me.

Ella, however, just gave me one of her *Jon Whitcroft, you're really getting all worked up about nothing* looks that I would come to recognize all too well.

"Well, looks like you're in trouble," she said, pushing back her chair. And without looking around once more, she returned to the table where her friends were eating.

I must have looked particularly stupid as I stared after her, because Stu and Angus exchanged a worried glance before they set their trays down on my table.

"Don't tell me you're seeing ghosts down here as well," Stu said.

"Yes, you'd better watch out. There's one on the chair you're about to sit on," I growled back at him.

Ella got up to return her tray to the kitchen. I nodded in her direction. "Does either one of you know that girl? The one with the long dark hair?"

Angus looked at her and lowered his voice. "That's Ella Littlejohn. Her grandmother does ghost tours for tourists. My dad says the old lady's a real witch. I mean, she's supposed to have tame toads in her garden and everything!"

Stu snorted disdainfully.

"What's so funny?" Angus hissed. Ella was walking out of the dining hall with some of her friends. "Dad says her grandmother has put a curse on at least four people."

"Your dad also said Stonehenge was built by aliens."

"No, he didn't."

"Yes, he did."

I left the two to their fight and looked out the window. Just a few more hours and it would be dark again.

Well, looks like you're in trouble.

"I...eh...have to go," I muttered. I ignored Stu's curious look and ran after Ella.

I found her outside, even though it had started raining again. She was leaning against a tree, looking at the cathedral. She didn't seem very surprised to see me.

48

"My grandmother says there's a Gray Lady in the cathedral," she said as I sidled up to her. "But I only ever saw the boy who haunts the cloisters. He's a mason's apprentice who fell off the scaffolding while they were finishing the tower." She caught a raindrop with the tip of her tongue. "He likes to scare the tourists. Whispers old swear words and such things. Quite silly, really, but he's probably just bored. I think most ghosts are bored."

That seemed to be a pretty bad excuse for hunting eleven-year-old boys across the Cathedral Close. But I kept that opinion to myself.

The rain had darkened the walls of the cathedral, and it now looked as if it were built out of the gray skies themselves. Until then I'd pretty much ignored the cathedral, together with everything else that brought the tourists to Salisbury. But I hadn't forgotten that on the evening before, it had seemed like the only safe place in the whole damn city. (See? I also like to swear when I'm scared.) So I felt particularly disheartened when I heard that there were also ghosts behind those

walls, even if those ghosts were merely dead apprentices, not hanged men.

"I...eh..." I wiped a few raindrops from my nose. Ever since my arrival in Salisbury, rain had been falling so often that it felt as if the whole world were being dissolved in water. "I heard about your grandmother. Do you think...I mean...could she maybe help me?"

Ella pushed her wet hair behind her ear and looked at me thoughtfully. "Possible," she said. "She knows a lot about ghosts. I've only seen a few, but Zelda's met dozens."

Dozens! The world was obviously a much more worrying place than I had thought. Until then the worst I had ever encountered was a bearded dentist.

"You're a boarder, right?" Ella asked. "Just ask the Popplewells if you can come visit us. Or do you go home on weekends?"

Home. Going there would have meant being forever marked as the homesick crybaby who made up stories about ghosts so he could go back to his mum. I hear you ask, *And? Definitely better than being dead.* But I already had that pride thing back then — not to mention that I couldn't stand the neighbor who was looking after the dog and my sisters.

"No," I mumbled. "Not going home."

"Great." Ella caught another raindrop on her tongue. She was as tall as I, even though she was a year behind me. "Then I'll tell my gran you're coming by tomorrow."

"Tomorrow? But that's too late. What if they come back tonight?" The panic in my voice was embarrassingly obvious, but I could still hear that hollow whisper in my head: *The hare always ends up dead.*

Ella frowned. "I told you they can't *do* anything to you. They can't even touch you. The only way ghosts can hurt you is through your own fear."

Great! I definitely had more than enough of that.

My desperation was obviously still splashed all over my face, because Ella sighed. "All right!" she said. "Then come by today. But no later than half past four. Zelda takes her nap at five, and she gets terribly ratty if her nap is disturbed."

She fished a pen out of her jacket pocket and took

my arm. "We're in number seven," she said as she wrote the street name on my arm. "Just take the path through the sheep meadows. Our house is right behind the old mill. But don't step on the toads. My grandmother loves them more than anything."

Toads. Angus's father had been right about that. Whatever. A raindrop smudged one of the letters on my arm. I quickly pulled my sleeve down over it. Ella's handwriting was quite pretty. Of course.

"Do you live with your grandmother?" I asked.

"Only when my parents are on tour."

"On tour?"

"Second violin and flute. They play in an orchestra. But it's not a very good one." She turned around. "See you at four thirty," she called over her shoulder.

I looked after her as she ran toward the school building.

Four ghosts and a witch's granddaughter. *Can't get crazier than that,* I thought. But of course I was wrong about that as well.

5

An Old Murder

There was only one way I could speak to Ella's grandmother before her afternoon nap: I had to steal away during homework period. I'd get into quite a lot of trouble, but the hope of getting rid of the four ghosts made it worth any detention. At around ten past four, I squeezed myself through the window of the boys' bathroom. I nearly ran into Bonapart on the path leading to the gate, but luckily he was so lost in thought that he didn't notice me.

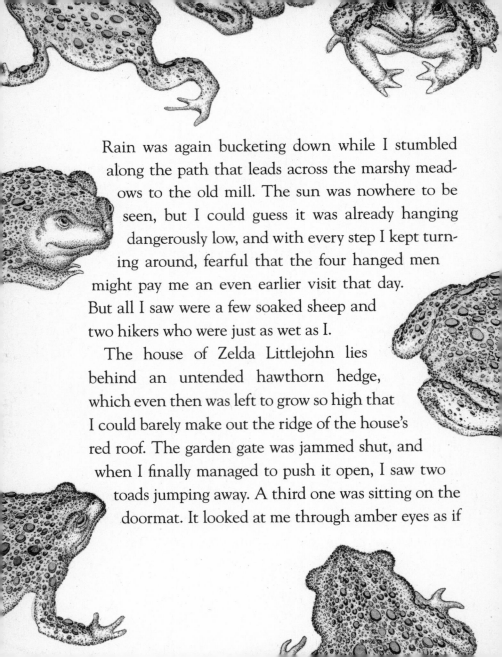

Rain was again bucketing down while I stumbled along the path that leads across the marshy meadows to the old mill. The sun was nowhere to be seen, but I could guess it was already hanging dangerously low, and with every step I kept turning around, fearful that the four hanged men might pay me an even earlier visit that day. But all I saw were a few soaked sheep and two hikers who were just as wet as I.

The house of Zelda Littlejohn lies behind an untended hawthorn hedge, which even then was left to grow so high that I could barely make out the ridge of the house's red roof. The garden gate was jammed shut, and when I finally managed to push it open, I saw two toads jumping away. A third one was sitting on the doormat. It looked at me through amber eyes as if

it had never seen anything as strange as I. It uttered a croak as I pushed the slightly rusty doorbell, and when Ella opened the door, it tried to jump past her and into the house. But Ella was faster; she caught the toad with a practiced hand.

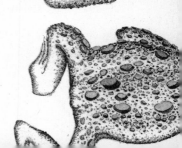

"You should be ashamed of yourself!" she said, looking sternly at the wildly kicking creature. "After what happened this morning, you're all banned from the house for at least a month."

She put her prisoner into a big pot next to the door. Two other toads were already sitting in it. Ella put a cloth over the pot.

"My grandmother nearly stepped on one this morning," Ella said, gesturing at me to follow her into the

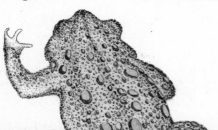

house. "She sprained her foot trying not to squash it. I keep telling Zelda she shouldn't let them into the house, but she won't listen."

As we walked past the living room, I spotted two more toads sitting on the sofa. Ella followed my glance and sighed.

"Yes, I know. They're everywhere," she said, leading me down the corridor. The wallpaper was covered in sunflowers, which were big enough to make you dizzy. "Zelda says she keeps them only because they eat the slugs, but that's nonsense. The garden is full of slugs, despite all the toads. I heard that she was already crazy about them as a child and that she kept bringing them to school."

I was wondering what Bonapart would have said about a toad on his desk, but before I could picture the scene, Ella stopped in front of a door.

"The doctor said Zelda won't be able to do any tours for at least two weeks," she whispered. "So she's in quite a foul mood."

I braced myself for the worst. However, the old lady, who was lying on a bed and had a bandaged foot, did not seem very frightening. Zelda looked like an owl that had fallen from its nest. Her glasses seemed far too big for her little wrinkly face, and her short gray hair looked like ruffled feathers. Like her granddaughter, Zelda didn't much go for greetings or introductions.

"That him?" was all she asked as she eyed me through her thick glasses.

"Be nice to him!" Ella replied. She sat down at the foot end of the bed. "His name's Jon, and the ghosts have already freaked him out enough."

Zelda, however, just snorted disdainfully and kept eyeing me so suspiciously that I started to blush. She could probably read from my face that I thought her granddaughter was the prettiest girl in the whole school.

"Didn't you say he saw *four* ghosts?" Zelda asked, reaching for the coffee mug on her bedside table. "That boy looks as pale as if he's seen at least a dozen! Unusual for them to appear in groups," she observed before taking a sip of coffee. "Most ghosts are loners."

"Ella . . . Ella said you've met quite a few?" I muttered.

"Oh yes! I see them everywhere. No idea why they

love to show themselves to me. I don't even like them! The first one I saw was my grandfather. One morning he was sitting on my bed, and I got to listen to him complaining about my grandmother's new hairdo. I usually advise people to ignore them, but Ella tells me that the four you saw have become quite unpleasant. So why don't you tell me what exactly they did, and I'll tell you how to get rid of them."

Zelda didn't interrupt me while I told her about the riders under my window and the chase across the Cathedral Close. She just drank her coffee and raised her eyebrows a few times. (Zelda's eyebrows were as dark as Ella's, though the grandmother surely had to use dye to maintain that color.) It was only when I got to the bit at the cathedral that she suddenly frowned.

"He called you *Hartgill*?"

"Yes. That's my mother's maiden name. But I have no idea how they could know that."

Zelda put her mug back on the bedside table. "Get me those crutches the doctor left this morning!" she said to Ella.

"But you're not supposed to get up!" Ella protested.

"The crutches! Now!"

Ella shrugged and did as she was told. Her grandmother cursed the pain as she hobbled down the corridor. I soon learned Zelda always swears using strange plant names: *stinkwort, nettlemuck, skunkbush, sumac.* She seemed to have an endless supply of those. Zelda hobbled into her living room. On shelves next to the door were boxes with labels such as FEMALE GHOSTS OF SALISBURY, POLTERGEISTS OF WILTSHIRE, GHOST STORIES OF SOUTHWEST ENGLAND, and HAUNTED HOUSES IN SUSSEX.

"Ella!" Zelda ordered, pointing at one of the boxes on the lowest shelf. Ella pulled it out, giving me a worried look. I didn't like the label either: DARK TALES.

Zelda sank into her sofa with a suppressed "Stinkbane!" Then she started flicking through the index cards in the box with a deep frown on her forehead. Finally she pulled out a card. "There we are. *Hartgill.* I had a feeling I'd seen that name somewhere!" she mumbled. Then she gave a deep sigh.

61

"What?" I asked in a failing voice.

"Heavens, Jon!" Zelda said. "Why did your parents have to send you to school in Salisbury, of all places? This was bound to happen. Kilmington is barely an hour from here."

"K-Kilmington?" I stammered. "Uh—"

Zelda cut me off. "Call your mother. Tell her she has to send you to another school. As far away from Salisbury as possible."

One of the toads on the sofa croaked, as if seconding Zelda's suggestion. I felt my knees go as soft as toad spawn.

"F-far away? Does that mean there's nothing you can do about them?"

Zelda swiped the two toads off the sofa and gave the card to Ella.

"There. Read this to him. I think I know who's hunting him."

Ella looked at the card with a frown.

"*Lord Stourton*," she read, "*hanged March 6, 1556, on Salisbury's Market Square, with a silken rope, in deference* to his noble blood. *The claims that Stourton was buried in Salisbury Cathedral are wrong, even if there are stories that describe the apparition of a noose above the crypt; those have been wrongly attributed to him. He was buried together with his four servants, and he's said to be haunting the graveyard in Kilmington.*"

Ella put down the card, and Zelda gave me a quizzical look.

"Does that sound like them?"

Maybe. My hand involuntarily touched my neck. *Lord Stourton*...Giving a name to my pursuer didn't really help.

"But why is he after Jon?" Ella asked.

"Read on," Zelda replied.

Ella picked up the card again. "*Stourton and his servants were hanged for the murder of*"—she caught her breath and looked at me—"*William Hartgill and his son John.*"

Zelda took off her glasses and polished them with the hem of her blouse. The flowers on it were nearly as bad as those on the wallpaper. "That should explain

why your ghost isn't very keen on the Hartgills, don't you think?" she said. "Hartgill was Stourton's steward, and Stourton tried several times to kill him. Terrible story. John Hartgill saved his father twice, but in the end Stourton lured them both into a trap and killed them. It was a horrific murder, even by the standards of those times."

There was another croak from behind the sofa.

"Stinkwort! There's another one!" Zelda groaned, peering over the back of the sofa. "I think I may have to get rid of the little beasts. Maybe I should take them all to the millpond and—"

"Zelda!" Ella interrupted sternly. "Forget about the toads. What about Jon? There *has* to be a way to get rid of these ghosts! Just like you got rid of that headless woman who used to sit in your brother's kitchen. Or the poltergeist from the old mill . . ."

"Balderdash! Nobody 'got rid of him'. It just got too noisy for him there!" Zelda put her glasses back on. "And Stourton's a ghost of a different caliber. The stories about him are the spookiest you'll find for miles around."

"Spooky?" I whispered.

"Yes, but don't put too much stock in those, boy." Zelda tried hard to sound calm. "People around here talk a lot when it gets dark. Most of it is foolish twaddle — though those stories are pure gold when it comes to my tours."

"What stories? Come on, tell us." Ella could really sound quite stern.

"As I said, nothing but twaddle!" Zelda groaned as she rubbed her bandaged foot. "That dead lord has been blamed for a few strange deaths in the area, and people always manage to bend it so that the victims were all male Hartgills."

"D-d-deaths?" I stuttered. "But . . . but Ella said ghosts can't really harm you!"

"Yes, and that is true!" Zelda said in a very firm voice. "I told you . . . twaddle. Over in Kilmington they claim that Stourton has a pack of black demon hounds that chase his victims to death. And here in Salisbury we have that story of the chorister whom Stourton supposedly threw out a window in your school, just for being very distantly related to the Hartgills. It's all nonsense! Ghosts are annoying, and sometimes they can be quite frightening, but it's as Ella said—in the end they're all completely harmless."

Harmless? I could still hear that hoarse voice in my head, and I felt the blade of his sword on my neck. *Harmless* was definitely not how I would have described him.

Ella also seemed unconvinced by what Zelda had said. She was still frowning at the card in her hand. "What if the stories are true?" she asked. "What if those ghosts really *can* kill Jon?"

Zelda uttered a curse as she pushed herself up from the sofa. It sounded something like "thistlecrap."

"Don't worry, my darling," she said. "They won't harm a hair on his head, no matter how scary they seem. They are dead, and all they want is a little bit of attention. But if I were Jon, I'd still find myself another school. That Stourton fellow is supposed to be quite a persistent ghost. Jon probably won't be getting much sleep if he stays in Salisbury. Come!" she said. "Help me get back to the bedroom. This foot is going to drive me mad, I can tell already. Maybe I should ask the doctor to saw it off. Isn't that what they do in the movies?"

Zelda held out her arm, but Ella didn't move. She can also be quite stubborn.

"What if they come back tonight?" she asked.

Zelda looked at me.

"Ignore them!" she answered. "They hate that. And stay away from open windows—you never know." Then she held out her arm again. But Ella still wasn't moving.

"Zelda, what about the *knight*?" she asked. "Don't you always say he's just waiting to be called to someone's aid?"

Zelda dropped her arm again. "Heavens, Ella! That's just another one of those stories I tell the tourists. You know I tell them a lot of things that aren't true."

"You also told that story to my mother. As a bedtime story. And she told it to me."

"Because it's a great story. But nobody has ever seen him."

"Because nobody has ever called him."

I had no idea what they were talking about. I just knew that I was still scared. So terribly scared that I felt quite sick. I could see the millpond through Zelda's living-room window. It reflected the gray afternoon sky. Just a few more hours and it would be dark again. Where would the ghosts be waiting for me this time?

Ella and Zelda were still arguing.

"Well, then..." I mumbled, turning toward the door. "Thanks."

A toad was sitting in front of the door. I caught it and put it in the pot with the others. Then I stepped outside and pulled the door shut behind me.

What now?

Back to the school, what else, Jon? I thought. Maybe you could say you spent the whole of study hall in the bathroom. Mrs. Cunningham is quite gullible. And then you could call your mother.

As I walked toward Zelda's gate, I worked on the

speech I would give my mother. *"Mum, Ella's grandmother says you have to send me to another school. Have you ever heard of Lord Stourton? No, this has nothing to do with me being homesick—and also nothing to do with The Beard."*

"Yeah, right!" I muttered as I pulled Zelda's gate shut behind me. "She won't believe a word."

I turned into the path that leads through the meadows. I heard steps behind me.

"Where are you going?" Ella planted herself in front of me.

"Where do you think?" I replied. "I have to get back to school. Maybe I won't get into too much trouble if I manage to get there before supper."

Ella shook her head. "No, you're not. We're going to the cathedral."

"The cathedral? Why?"

Ella just took my arm and dragged me along.

As I said, Ella never makes too many words.

6

A Long-Forgotten Oath

When Ella and I walked back into the Cathedral Close, the old houses were already blurring into the twilight. Hardly any tourists were in front of the cathedral, even though the gates to the close aren't locked until ten p.m. Not for the first time did it seem to me that the Cathedral Close of Salisbury had been forgotten by time. Only the parked cars indicated that we were still in the same century we'd been in at Zelda's house.

The cathedral rose into the sky as if trying to reach the darkening clouds with its tower. Again the walls seemed to offer protection from all that was evil in the world. But how? I couldn't just spend the rest of the school year hiding in an old church.

"Ella? What exactly are we doing here?" I asked as I followed her across the lawn where Stourton had caught up with me and where I had sunk to my knees in front of Bonapart. Through a row of trees to our left, I could see the walls of the school, where Mrs. Cunningham had probably already reported me to the headmaster.

"We're going to visit someone who can help you," Ella said. "Or have you changed your mind about calling your mother?"

She managed to make that option sound even more embarrassing than it already was.

"No," I barked at her. "No. Of course not." And I decided not to ask any more questions for the time being.

We took the cloister entrance, which is the one most

tourists use. The stone arches cast long shadows, and on the garth—the lawn enclosed by them—a huge cedar held the darkness between its branches, just as it had done for nearly two centuries.

By all those saints staring down at us from the roof—whom did Ella want to meet here? Was she going to ask one of the priests to drive Stourton away? Or one of the stone angels? I looked between the pillars for the dead apprentice, but Ella was waving me along impatiently toward the entrance to the cathedral.

The air behind the heavy doors was so chilly it made me shiver, and the twilight between the gray walls wrapped itself around me like a protective blanket, even though I suddenly remembered the Gray Lady Ella had mentioned earlier.

Ella bought tickets for us and then led me down the central aisle toward the altar. Behind it, in the choir stalls, Angus sung hymns every day, the ones he kept humming in his sleep. Around us the columns rose up like trees. High above, the spandrels that held up the

ceiling spread out as if the columns were growing branches of stone. The huge church was nearly empty; fewer than a dozen visitors were scattered among the aisles. Our steps rang out in the silence, and for a moment I thought I could hear all the footsteps of all the visitors who'd ever come to the church over the centuries to ask for help and salvation.

Ella stopped. In front of us were the four bent pillars that support the roof of the cathedral's tower. They really are bent. Some bishop hundreds of years ago decided that the cathedral of Salisbury was going to be the first church in the world with a pointy roof. The additional load had nearly collapsed the tower. But Ella was not leading me to the bent pillars. Instead, she dragged me to a sarcophagus in front of them to our right. The last rays of daylight were falling through the high windows, painting colorful shadows on the well-worn flagstones.

"There he is!" Ella whispered.

There was who?

A knight, sleeping on the sarcophagus. He was

stretched out on the stone coffin, his face turned sideways. The face was barely visible under his helmet. A sign next to the sarcophagus explained that the effigy had once been painted, but time had bleached the colors away and had turned the stone limbs as pale white as the bones of a dead man.

"His name is William Longspee," Ella whispered. "He was the bastard son of Henry the Second and the half brother of Richard the Lionheart. He can help you against Stourton. You just have to call him."

I stared down at the chiseled face.

That's what she brought me here for? The disappointment nearly choked me. Yes, of course. The past two nights had definitely convinced me for good that the dead could be very alive. But this? This was nothing more than a figure chiseled out of stone.

"There's also a monument to his son in the cathedral," Ella whispered. "But he's buried in Israel, because he died on a Crusade. Zelda says they hacked him to pieces. Disgusting."

Outside, the day was dying. Darkness flooded the

cathedral. Stourton and his servants were probably waiting for me already.

"No way, Ella!" I hissed. "Is that the knight you asked Zelda about?"

"Yes. I'm positive the stories about him are true. It's just that nobody has called him in a long time. And you have to really need his help, or he won't appear."

Two women stopped next to us and began to discuss the sculptural qualities of Longspee's tomb. Ella glowered at them until they fell into an awkward silence and finally walked off.

As soon as we were alone again, Ella whispered, "I wrote an essay about him. He's said to have sworn an oath when he returned from the war." She lowered her voice. "*I, William Longspee, will not find peace until I have cleansed my soul from all my sinful deeds. For this I will protect the innocent from the cruel, and the weak from the strong. This I swear, so help me God.* But then he died, and some people say he's still trying to fulfill his oath."

Ella gave me an encouraging look.

"What?" I whispered. "This is totally crazy. Not all the dead come back, Ella!"

At least that's what I hoped.

Ella rolled her eyes and looked around as if asking for the aid of all the saints around us.

"Do you have another idea?" she whispered. "Who can better protect you from ghosts than another ghost?"

"That's *not* an idea!" I hissed back. "That's just crazy."

But Ella was ignoring me. She had turned around. More and more people were coming down the central aisle. Of course. The choristers would soon start the evensong, and Angus would be among them. What if he told the Popplewells that he saw me in the cathedral?

I took Ella's arm and quickly pulled her between the pillars behind Longspee's tomb.

"Your knight is probably not even buried here!" I said quietly, leaning against the gray stone. "Or didn't

Bonapart tell you that they kept moving the graves around? Sometimes they lost the bones, or even mixed them up!"

There. The choristers, wearing their blue robes, appeared behind the rows of chairs. Angus was one of the first ones. As usual, he had his finger in the stiff white collar. He kept moaning about how the thing choked him.

"Well, that's definitely William Longspee in that grave," Ella hissed while the choristers, followed by the priests, filed past us toward the altar. "You know why? Because when they moved the tomb to this place, they found a dead rat in his skull. You can see it in the museum."

I suppressed a wave of nausea and tried to look unimpressed. "And?"

Ella sighed at so much ignorance. "Longspee died so suddenly that everybody was convinced he'd been poisoned. But nobody could prove anything until they found the rat. It was full of arsenic."

She obviously loved that story. I didn't. Murderers

and the murdered. What had happened to my life? I briefly pictured The Beard on top of a sarcophagus, bleached and turned to stone. But one glance at the dark church windows reminded me that I had other things to worry about.

Behind the altar, the altar boys were lighting the candles, and outside Stourton was just now probably picking the window through which he'd throw me. And I was talking to a girl I hardly knew about dead knights and poisoned rats.

"You have to call him!" Ella whispered. "As soon as we're alone."

The choristers began to sing. Their voices rang through the dark church as if the stones themselves were joining the song.

"Alone? And how is that going to happen?" I whispered back. "The cathedral is locked after evening mass."

"And? We get ourselves locked in."

"Locked in?" This just kept getting worse.

Ella took my hand. She pulled me down the north

aisle. Behind me I could hear Angus start the solo for which he had practiced every morning in the washroom. Ella stopped in front of a door made of dark wood studded with iron nails. She pushed down the handle, cast a quick glance to the left and right, and then opened the door. The room behind it was barely more than a cupboard. Ella pushed me inside and closed the door behind us.

"Perfect, isn't it?" I heard her whisper. "A chorister showed it to me once."

"What for?" Being so close to her in a dark room made me very nervous.

"He wanted to kiss me." The disgust in Ella's voice was obvious. "But luckily, I'm stronger than any one of them."

I was glad she couldn't see me blush in the darkness. I had just pictured what it would feel like to touch her hair.

We could hear the choristers even through the closed door. Angus always claimed he could shatter glass with his voice, though he had never been able to prove it to me or Stu.

"Sounds nice, doesn't it?" Ella whispered.

I wasn't so sure. Ever since The Beard had marched into my life, I'd started to like loud music, very loud music, and definitely not Peace on Earth. This made me wonder even more how Angus, who always got into fights and who lost his temper in every rugby match, could produce such angelic harmonies and even enjoy it. "How can you walk around in that stupid outfit?" I'd asked him when I first saw him put on his robe (I had just failed my chorister audition). "Whitcroft, you have no idea!" Angus had answered, giving me a sympathetic smile as he brushed some dog hairs from the blue cloth. He was probably right, and not only about the choristers' gowns. His statement was definitely true when it came to girls too. And that was exactly why waiting in that dark room with Ella made me nearly as uncomfortable as Stourton's hollow whispers.

"Yes. Doesn't sound bad," I mumbled. I quickly pulled

back the elbow that had accidentally brushed against Ella's arm. *What are you doing here, Jon Whitcroft? I* thought. *Are you really going to make a complete ass of yourself by trying to wake a dead knight?*

The evensong lasted less than an hour, though it felt to me as if a year had passed before the choristers and the organ finally fell silent and we heard the sound of footsteps and laughter.

They were leaving.

We heard the doors being shut and the solitary steps of the priest who extinguished the lights. And then silence.

We were alone in the cathedral.

Alone with the dead.

7

THE DEAD KNIGHT

Ella opened the door. The air smelled of molten
wax, and the song of the choristers seemed to
linger between the columns.

The darkness only made the cathedral feel bigger. It
was as if the night had brought the place to life, its very
own kind of life, and it wouldn't have surprised me to
see one of the saints step off his pedestal to ask us what
in the devil's name (well, probably more like what in
God's name) we were doing there at that time of night.

Yes, what? *Making fools of ourselves!* I thought as Ella pushed a flashlight into my hand. She obviously had no doubts about her plan.

"What do you think?" she asked, letting the beam of her flashlight run down the row of columns. "Shall we wait until midnight? Zelda says that's still the time most ghosts prefer to appear."

"Midnight?" I looked at my watch.

Midnight was *five* hours away!

"You're right!" Ella said. "Why wait? Let's call him now. Come on!"

Think of Stourton, Jon! I thought as I stumbled after her. *This can't make things any worse.*

Outside, the moon had found a tiny gap in the clouds. Its light fell on Longspee's effigy, making the stone look as white as snow. He really looked as if he were just asleep.

Ella nodded at me encouragingly before stepping back.

Come on, Jon. You have to at least try, or she'll never forgive you.

I stepped closer to the sarcophagus. I would have needed just to lift my hand to touch Longspee's glove.

"Jon!" Ella whispered behind me. "He's a knight. You have to kneel!"

Kneel?

Whatever. I went down to my knees.

"My name...um...is Jon Whitcroft."

My voice seemed to get lost in the silence, and no matter how much I tried to make it deeper, it still was the squeaky voice of a kid.

"I...I'm here to ask for your help. Somebody wants to kill me. And because he's as dead as you, Ella thought..."

I stopped. No. This was just too stupid. The flagstones were as cold as ice, and the moon still made Longspee's face look as white as a corpse. As if it wanted to remind me that I was kneeling in front of a dead man. I longed to go home and forget about everything that had happened in the past months—including Stourton and The Beard.

But when I got to my feet, I heard Ella whisper

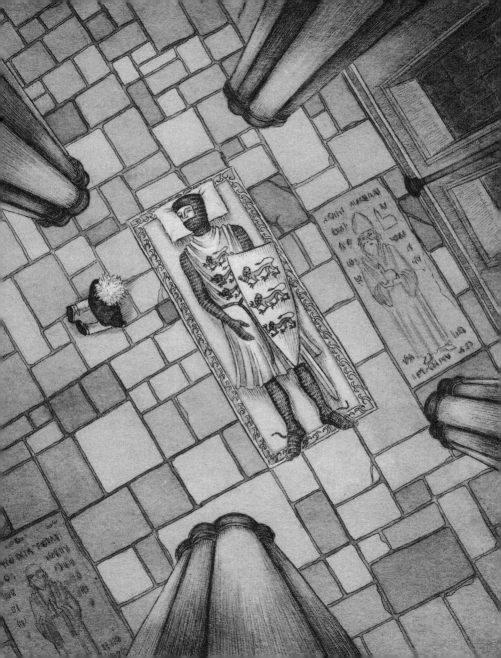

behind me: "What are you doing? Stay where you are. Don't you know anything about knights? They used to kneel like that for hours."

Yep, I had heard about that.

I could smell the autumn flowers on the altar, and I thought of the four murderers with the broken necks, of William Hartgill and his son, and I thought that I didn't really want a new father.

"Please!" I heard myself whisper. The words came out by themselves. "Please, William Longspee, help me."

Suddenly I heard steps. Rattling steps, as if made by iron shoes.

I turned around.

And there he was.

Whenever I close my eyes, I can still see him as clearly as on that night. And it will always be that way.

The tunic covering Longspee's chain-mail shirt showed the three lions of Salisbury on a background of blue and gold. Unlike in his stone image, he was not wearing a helmet. His face was beardless, his eyes pale blue. His short ash-blond hair showed no signs of graying.

"Get up, boy!" he said. "I remember how stiff legs could get from all that kneeling. I would assist you, but since I cannot offer you a hand of flesh and blood, I'd be little help to you."

It really wasn't that easy getting back to my feet. But that was because my knees were shaking, which I hoped he didn't notice.

The knight was taller than I'd expected, and his chain mail shimmered as if the moon itself had made the armor for him.

He looked so glorious. Just like the knights I had dreamed about when I was six years old, whacking at the brambles in our garden, imagining I was fighting dragons and giants with a sword that made me invincible and wearing armor that protected me from all the things that frightened me — older kids, dogs, a storm in the night, or my little sister's questions about when our father would be coming back.

I managed a clumsy bow. I didn't know what else I

was supposed to do. All I knew was that my fear was gone — as if Longspee had wiped it off my soul.

He smiled, but the smile was only on his lips. His eyes looked as if he hadn't had much occasion to smile during the past centuries.

"It has been a long time since someone asked me for help," he said in a voice that seemed to come from far away. "I nearly did not hear you. I have dark dreams. They now rarely let me go. I am afraid you may have found the wrong knight." He pointed to a sarcophagus a few steps away on the other side of the aisle. The chiseled knight on it looked like a giant.

"His name is Cheney," Longspee said. "He has a temper, and he likes to be paid for his services. But I am sure that if you put a few coins on his brow, he will come to your aid."

He looked around as if he'd forgotten where he was.

"Let me sleep, Jon Whitcroft," he said, his voice weary and tired. "When the shadows of your life haunt you, and you bitterly miss the ones you once loved, then only sleep can grant oblivion."

His features began to blur like a photograph that's out of focus. His whole body began to fade.

No!

I wanted to reach for his gloved hand and hold on to him, but I just stood there and felt fear flood back—the fear, the loneliness, and the anger—while Longspee's shimmering body dissolved into the darkness. Of course. Nothing but a hallucination, brewed from fear and homesickness and from Bonapart's constant babbling about the Lionheart.

"But it is *you* he called, not Cheney."

Ella's voice sounded very loud in the deserted cathedral. I had all but forgotten about her.

For a moment there was silence. Then Longspee's voice came through the darkness as if he was standing behind one of the columns.

"I see you have not come alone, Jon Whitcroft."

"No, this is...Ella," I stuttered. "It was her idea to call you."

"Ella?" Longspee said her name as if he wanted to

savor every letter on his tongue. His shape became clearer again.

"Yes." Ella stepped to my side. "Like your wife. Ella Longspee. But in Lacock Abbey, where she's buried, they call her Ela. What did *you* call her?"

Longspee's shape shuddered like a reflection on dark water.

"*Ella*," he answered. "I always called her Ella. Since the moment I saw her for the first time. She was then probably not much older than you, but her hair was blond, and she was not as tall as you. Even as a grown woman, she barely reached up to my shoulder. And yet she was stronger than any man I knew in my lifetime."

Ella brushed back her hair. She always does that when she's self-conscious, though back then I didn't know that yet.

"Yes, that's what my mother told me about her. She named me after your wife."

Longspee scrutinized Ella's face as if, despite all the differences, it made him see the face of another.

Then he looked at me again. "I wonder how long I have slept this time. Time passes slowly when you fear hell and don't yet deserve heaven." He ran his hands along the hilt of his sword. I briefly thought I could see blood on his hands and his clothes. But as he turned, those stains were washed away by the moonlight.

"And what help do you desire from a dead knight, Jon?"

As I told Longspee about Stourton and his servants, the whole cathedral seemed to be listening, all the saints and all the dead sleeping in their tombs. Longspee listened with an impassive face, as though he really was the stone effigy brought to life. A few times Ella filled in some gaps, but eventually we both fell silent. Longspee looked up at the windows as if he could see my pursuers standing outside under the stars.

"I know those kinds of men," he finally said. "They are poison, on either side of death. Which is not to say that I myself did not fight for them in my lifetime." As he looked down the row of columns, it seemed as if he could see a memory from his life behind each one. "There are four? And they only come to you by night?"

I nodded.

"I've only seen four, but I know Stourton was buried with another servant. They say they will hunt me until I am dead. Ella's grandmother says they can't hurt me, but..." My voice faltered.

Longspee looked at me. Then he took off his left glove.

"Hold out your hand, Jon Whitcroft," he said.

I did.

Shimmering on Longspee's middle finger was the ghostly pale image of a ring. The coat of arms on it was hazy, again like a faded photograph. But when Longspee pressed the ring into the palm of my hand, it burned like ice and left the imprint of a lion on my skin.

"The next time you see Stourton," said Longspee, "close your fist over my crest, and I will be there."

Then he stepped back and disappeared. It was as if

the cathedral had taken a deep breath and made him part of itself again. Even the moonlight vanished, as if Longspee had taken it with him. Ella and I stood there and looked at each other. We could hardly see each other in the darkness, but it didn't matter. I could still see Ella's broad smile. And she, of course, found exactly the right words.

"There you go!" she whispered.

We went to sleep right next to William's sarcophagus. As I was drifting off, I thought I could see a Gray Lady walk down the central aisle of the cathedral. But maybe I was already dreaming. Stourton did not show up that night. That's all I know. And I felt as safe next to the stone coffin as if I were back at home, in my orphaned bed.

NOT SUCH A BAD AFTERNOON

A priest found Ella and me the next morning. I had slept well for the first time in days, and the lion mark on my hand proved that Longspee hadn't been just a dream. When I got back to school and Mrs. Cunningham, looking very aggrieved, asked me about my disappearance, I muttered a few touching sentences about my mother's horrid new boyfriend and that I'd hoped saying a few prayers in the cathedral might make him disappear. (I know, I should've been struck down by a thunderbolt from the tower, but the heavens probably have some compassion for jealous sons.) I apologized a dozen times to Mrs. Cunningham and to the Popplewells, who had been out most of the night searching for me. I swore a most holy oath never again to climb through the bathroom window during homework period.

When you're eleven, you know exactly what adults want to hear, and I do admit I was proud that my story was accepted with a pat on the shoulder (from the headmaster) and two tearful embraces (one each from Mrs. Cunningham and Alma Popplewell). The truth probably wouldn't have had anywhere near the same effect. A kid who tried to drive off his mother's lover through prayer is much less disconcerting than the appearance of a dead knight.

Happily, my only punishment was an essay about the importance of rules and their observance, as well as detention for the rest of the weekend, to be spent under the supervision of the Popplewells. Ella was not at all happy when she heard about it. After all, she wanted to be there when Longspee sent Stourton to hell. She'd already convinced Zelda to let both of us sleep in her house, in the hope that my pursuers might turn up there. And now my detention had ruined her beautiful plan.

Ella hadn't gotten detention. Zelda had accepted her story that she'd found me in the cathedral in such a pitiful state and that she'd spent hours trying to calm me, during which time we'd gotten ourselves locked in.... Yes, I know, Zelda can be quite gullible.

Ella hadn't told her about Longspee.

"Why?" she repeated when I asked her about it. "Zelda would only want to meet him, and then she'd ask him all these questions about his life and his wife. She can be really embarrassing!"

Both Stu and Angus had gone home to their families for the weekend, so I spent the entire Saturday alone in our deserted room, staring at the mark on my hand and not knowing whether to anticipate or fear the coming evening.

Ella came to visit around four o'clock. She was still angry about my detention.

"Well, thanks a lot!" she said as we sat on the garden wall down by the river, feeding the ducks dry toast. It was a sunny day, which made for a nice change after all the recent rain. "So you get to have all the fun."

"Fun?" I asked. "Define fun. Longspee still has to deal with a bunch of ghosts. The next time you see me, I may be just as dead as he is."

Ella responded with one of her *Jon Whitcroft, how stupid do you think I am?* looks. And I admit I was actually feeling quite optimistic about William Longspee's qualities as a protector.

"I still need a good story about vanishing yesterday," I said, trying to change the subject. "The one about praying in the cathedral was great for the grown-ups, but if that story gets around the school, my reputation's going to be ruined for months."

"Easy," said Ella as she unwrapped the rolls Zelda had given her. (Her grandmother had stuck little onion-eyes on them, to make them look like toads.) "Tell them the truth. Just leave out the bit about Longspee. Say that I told you about the cupboard behind the door and that we never noticed the cathedral being locked up. You can tell them we kissed. Don't boys like to hear that stuff?"

I turned as red as the ketchup Zelda had put on the rolls. I could only mutter that nobody would believe that story.

"Of course they'll believe it," Ella said. "Boys are so stupid. With some exceptions," she added graciously.

We sat on the wall, looked at the river, and ate Zelda's toad-rolls in silence. Ella probably believed I was thinking about Stourton and Longspee, but I was picturing Stu's face when I'd tell him that I kissed Ella Littlejohn.

A few boys were playing football in the park on the other side of the river. Two swans drifted past, and an old man on a bench was sharing his ice-cream cone with his very fat dog. It wasn't a bad afternoon, and I remember thinking that Salisbury might not be such a bad place after all.

I touched the lion mark on my hand. The skin there still felt as if it were frozen.

"Ella?" I asked. "You believe that he will actually come, right?"

Ella licked some ketchup from her fingers.

" 'Course!" she said.

'Course.

I brushed an ant from my jeans.

"Longspee's wife...the other Ella...what do you know about her?"

"Quite a lot." Ella turned her face to the sun. "My mother is obsessed with her." She changed her voice: *"Ella, just imagine. She was the first female sheriff of Wiltshire! She was present when the Magna Carta was signed!"*

The wind blew her dark hair into her face.

"Lionheart married her to Longspee when she was very young. Mum says they were very happy, even though he was much older than she was. And they had eight children. But then William Longspee's ship sank, and they wanted her to marry again, because Ella was the Countess of Salisbury. She said, 'No, William is not dead. You'll see. He'll come back.' And she was right.

But when he finally returned, he died very quickly. So Ella took his heart and buried it in Lacock, and she did the same later with her son's heart. And then she became a nun."

The sun disappeared behind the trees. Shivering, I turned up the collar of my jacket. The garden behind us filled with shadows.

"Well, no wonder he looks so miserable," I muttered.

Ella gently brushed a wasp off her knee. "Zelda says all ghosts have sad stories that they just cannot bring to an end."

The old man got up and left with his dog. The swans drifted away, and the boys who'd been playing football were gone too. For a moment Ella and I seemed to be the only people in the world.

"I have to go," Ella said. "The doctor said I have to make sure Zelda doesn't hobble around too much. As if she listens to me!" She put her hand on my arm. "Stay away from open windows!"

I didn't really think a closed window would stop a ghost, but I nodded.

"Call me," she said. "Here, this is Zelda's number, and this is my parents'. They're coming home tomorrow." This time she wasn't writing on my arm but on a piece of paper. She put it in my hand and slid off the wall.

"Jon..."

Suddenly her voice was barely more than a whisper.

I put the paper in my pocket.

"What?" I turned around.

Two huge dogs were standing between Alma Popplewell's rose beds. The Popplewells didn't have a dog, let alone two that were as black as a hole in the night.

Ella bit her lip. It was the first time I ever saw her afraid.

"I *hate* dogs!" she whispered.

I didn't think those two beasts looked like real dogs, but I kept that thought to myself. Their fur stood on end like that of real dogs, but real dogs didn't have red eyes, nor were they usually as big as calves. Whatever they were, they now bared their fangs as if they'd heard what Ella had just said.

In Kilmington they claim that Stourton has a pack of

black demon hounds that chase
his victims to death.

If I remembered Zelda's
story, so would Ella. *What
can we do?* I looked around wildly, and without really
thinking, I grabbed two logs of the firewood Edward
Popplewell had stacked by the garden wall. "Here!" I
whispered, thrusting one of the logs at Ella. "My grandpa
has a nasty shepherd dog. When they attack, we'll ram
the wood into their mouths."

Ella gave me a terrified look, but she still took the
log. I could see she'd also realized that we were dealing
with more than just a pair of normal stray dogs.

"What are you waiting for?" she whispered. "Call Longspee!"

The dogs uttered a growl that made us start. Black fog rose from the ground where they were standing. It drifted through the garden in dirty shrouds, and it grew ever denser—until everything disappeared in it: the trees, the house, and the garden wall. All of Salisbury dissolved into darkness, and out of the shadows came the horses I already knew so well. They had all come: Lord Stourton and his four murderous servants, on the hunt for another Hartgill. Three came from the left; the fourth came with his master from where, just moments before, I could have seen the Popplewells' house.

"Jon!" Ella hissed. "What are you waiting for?"

Yes, what? *Five*, I heard a whisper inside my head. Five. What was one man going to do against five murderers? But I still closed my fist over the lion mark. The hounds were panting and looking up at their master, as if begging him for the order to attack.

William Longspee. Please, help me.

He appeared as soon as my fingers pressed down on the mark. His chain mail shimmered brightly and seemed to flood the darkness with light. The ghost horses shied back, and the hounds crouched down on the grass. Longspee drew his sword and positioned himself between us and the horsemen.

"And what have we here? Five murderers." He spoke without raising his voice. "Have you run out of game so that you have to hunt children?"

The pale horses snorted, and the darkness closed in around them like poisonous smoke.

"Get out of our way." Stourton's voice sounded hoarse, as if the noose that hung from his neck was still choking his throat. "Have you gotten lost in time? The days of the knights were already over when I still had flesh and blood on my bones."

"And what about *your* days?" Longspee replied. "I see they were ended by a silken rope. Not a very honorable death!"

The black hounds growled, feeling the rage of their master. Stourton bared his teeth as if he were one of them. I felt Ella trembling next to me. I was glad she was standing by my side, and still I wished her far away in Zelda's house, where the only danger was stumbling over a toad.

"Ah! *Now* I know who you are!" Stourton barked. His servants drove their horses to his side. "You are that royal bastard they buried in the cathedral. The Lionheart's little brother. What are you still doing here? I thought you ascended straight to heaven with that noble soul everybody said you had."

"And why are you not in hell yet?" Longspee didn't take his eyes off Stourton's servants. "I should have thought the way should be easy enough to find for a murderer like you, who beat his victims after binding their hands. Or did even the devil deny you?"

Stourton straightened himself in the saddle. His bloodless face glowed like a deadly flower, and the darkness caressed him with its black hands as if he were its lord.

"I will ride into hell like a king," he rasped. "But only when there are no more Hartgills walking this earth."

He raised a hand that was as bony as Death himself, and when his servants drew their swords, their blades were again dripping with blood. I thought I could hear Alma Popplewell calling my name somewhere in the distance. A world where housemothers and other harmless creatures existed suddenly seemed as far away as the moon. Longspee took a step back. I saw his hand close around the hilt of his sword. There were five. Five against one. I was suddenly so afraid for Longspee that I wanted to jump forward and stand by his side. But Ella held me back.

"Jon, don't!" she whispered.

That very moment Stourton spurred his horse, driving it toward Longspee.

I screamed as Stourton struck with his sword, but Longspee was quicker. He dodged the blade and rammed his sword into the hanged man's side. Stourton's horse reared up as its master fell. He dropped onto the wet grass, and I could see his black heart glowing like a lump of coal behind his ribs. He uttered a hoarse curse as he struggled back to his feet. Blood as ghostly pale as

his skin was running down his white clothes. He waved his approaching men away with an angry bark. The darkness gathered around him like a cloak. The black hounds crouched by his side, their fur bristling and their teeth bared.

William looked back at us. I wasn't sure what I saw in his face. Was there fear after death? If so, then he showed fear for us.

Stourton was still staggering, but he picked up his sword from the grass. His servants were waiting behind him.

"One more time. Get out of my way, you fool!" he hissed at Longspee. "The boy is mine. He belonged to me ever since his Hartgill blood put that noose around my neck."

The evening sun warmed my neck, but it belonged to another world. Its rays were smothered by the black fog hanging over the garden.

"Be gone," said Longspee in a calm voice. "Be gone and do not return."

Stourton replied with a scornful laugh. It sounded

like the barking of a dog. His mouth gaped open as if his pale parchment skin had torn.

"Rip him apart!" he yelled. His dogs immediately jumped at Longspee with bared fangs. The knight hacked off the head of the first one before it could dig its teeth into him. The second hound got hold of his arm, but Longspee rammed his sword into the creature's back. The beasts dissolved into the filthy fog. Their howls tore through my ears, and before I knew what was happening, Ella had already tackled me to the ground, wrapping her arms protectively around me. Above us, blades connected with a loud clangor. My skin went ice-cold.

Five against one.

I saw their blades deflected off Longspee's chain-mail shirt, piercing his shoulder, cutting into his thigh. I saw blood, wounds that closed again as if the light surrounding Longspee sealed them. Two of Stourton's servants fell when Longspee rammed his sword into where their hearts had once been. The darkness billowed out of their chests; it briefly took human form and then dissolved amid terrible screams. The knight split open the head of the third servant. It was the hamster face. His body crumbled like ash and was stirred up by a breeze. Stourton's face was blazing with rage as the dying day found its way back into the garden.

But Longspee's breathing was labored. He staggered as the last servant charged at him, and his left arm hung limp at his side.

I tore free from Ella to help him, but suddenly Stourton was standing over me. I stumbled backward. Ella came to my aid, the log still in her hand. Brave Ella, but what good would a piece of firewood be against an immortal killer? Stourton blew his foul breath into her face, and she fell back onto the grass. I heard myself scream with rage; I felt my fists clenching to strike his cruel visage. But Stourton just sneered at me as he raised his sword.

That's it, Jon Whitcroft, I heard myself in my head. *How are they going to make sense of your death? That you drowned yourself from too much homesickness? That you cut yourself into slices and choked yourself with black smoke, taking poor Ella Littlejohn with you?* I thought I could already feel Stourton's blade between my ribs. Ella was definitely wrong. Of course he could kill me. He was going to slice us up! But suddenly Stourton's eyes died like embers extinguished by a cold breeze, and his bony hands dropped his sword. Longspee's blade thrust out of his chest, its wrought steel as black as soot, and the hanged lord collapsed in front of my feet. Smoke rose from the wound in his chest, and his moans brushed my face like an icy hand, as if he were still trying to take me with him. And then he was gone, and all that was left was an empty shell, like the skin of a molted dragonfly.

My whole body was shaking; I couldn't stop it. Around me the dark fog lifted, and I could again see the boardinghouse at the end of the garden.

"Ella?" I said in a trembling voice.

I didn't dare turn around. I was too afraid I would find her dead on the grass behind me. My heart skipped with joy when I heard her voice next to me.

"Oh, that's disgusting!" she said. And there she was,

dry leaves in her hair and a few scratches on her forehead, but she was alive—and she was staring with
revulsion at Stourton's empty shell as it dissolved in
the evening sun.

The last rays of sunshine also made Longspee fade. I
could barely see him as he pushed his sword back into
its scabbard.

"Thank you!" I stammered. "Thanks. We..."

Longspee just nodded silently. He gave us the shadow
of a smile, and then he was gone.

The setting sun flooded the garden with red and
gold. I couldn't see a trace of the fight, except for a few
broken twigs and some enormous paw prints that were
branded into the grass.

I heard Alma Popplewell call, "Jon?" Her voice no
longer sounded as if it came from another planet.
"Jon!"

"Here! We're in the garden!" I called back, surprised
at how normal my voice sounded.

Ella's knees were probably just as wobbly as mine as
she walked back to the house.

"Your mother's on the phone, Jon!" Alma called toward us. "I can't believe you were in the garden. Did you see that smoke? I wonder who's been burning God-only-knows-what in their garden again."

Ella and I exchanged a quick look. We couldn't believe that Alma didn't see on our faces what had happened, but she only paused at seeing the leaves in Ella's hair and the mud on my jeans.

"There were two dogs," I said. "Horrible beasts. But we chased them away."

"Dogs?" Alma cast a worried look into the garden. "Oh! They sometimes chase the ducks in the park, and then they jump over the wall. They really should forbid people from taking them off the leash in the park. Use the phone in the office, Jon. Ella can try some of the dessert I just made."

Dessert. My mother on the phone. Life did go on.

After what had just happened, it felt very strange to answer questions like "Have you made any new friends?" and "How's the food?" Instead, I wanted to ask her, "Mum, did you have any idea how dangerous it would

121

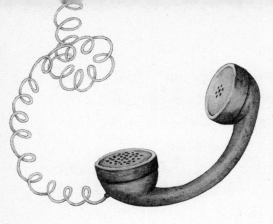

be for your son in Salisbury?" But I restrained myself. Longspee had sent Stourton to hell, and everything was okay.

My mother sounded happy. Her son had just survived an attempt on his life by a ghost lord, all because she sent him to what was the most dangerous place on earth to be a male member of her family, and she just talked about her vacation with The Beard and how nice he was being to my sisters. Never mind. I didn't care. I was just glad that I was alive and that nothing had happened to Ella. And that all this was now over.

"So, what do you say, Jon?"

Oops, I'd missed something.

"Say about what?"

"About a nice weekend for just the two of us? I'll come up next Friday and I'll stay until Sunday evening. You know, we have the builders in the house because

Matt urgently needs an office; otherwise I'd have loved to have you here. But don't you think it might be even nicer to have a few days just to ourselves? We could drive to Stonehenge, go for a walk, and have dinner in the Old Mill. We had only a few hours when we came to see the school, but this time we could also do the evensong in the cathedral. I've never been to the cathedral in the evening. It's probably magical, don't you think?"

"Probably," I mumbled, and I suddenly realized that I missed her terribly. I wanted to tell her everything that had happened to me in the past week (even though I was positive she wouldn't believe a word of it). I wanted her to meet Angus and Stu and Ella—yes, especially Ella. Though...maybe that wasn't such a good idea. Mothers can be embarrassing when they meet your friends, especially if the friends are girls. And suddenly the realization flashed through me like lightning. Hold on. She couldn't come. She was a

Hartgill, like me. *And?* asked the more reasonable part of my brain. Stourton was gone, dissolved, or whatever you called it when ghosts died. It was over. And hadn't Zelda said he was only after *male* Hartgills?

"Jon?"

I stared at the phone.

"Yes, I'm still here, Mum."

"Do you want me to come?"

"Sure." As long as The Beard didn't come as well....

Relax, Jon Whitcroft! It's over. No more dead murderers, no more black dogs. Now the only problem left in your life has a beard, and she said she wouldn't bring him. I looked at my hand. It was bleeding. I must have grazed it on the wall.

Ella poked her head through the door. She was holding two mugs of hot chocolate. Alma made excellent hot chocolate. Her desserts weren't quite so excellent.

"I'll call you during the week," my mother said, "as soon as I know which train I'm taking. Shall I bring you anything?"

"Sweets," I mumbled, still staring at my injured hand.

"Chocolate, licorice, gummy bears…" All of which were forbidden in the domain of the Popplewells, but she didn't have to know that. Maybe Angus could lend me one of his cuddly toys to hide my stash in.

Ella raised her eyebrows when she heard my list. She despised gummy bears and licorice — which was perfect. When you're eleven, there's nothing worse than having a friend who likes the same sweets as you.

Alma let Ella stay for the movie that was showing in the common room. It was some old horror flick with ghosts that looked like floating bedsheets. It wouldn't have scared even a second grader. But Ella and I couldn't laugh about it. We sat next to each other and tried to forget the ghosts we'd just met in the garden. And yet we both knew that we'd still remember them when we'd be as old as Zelda.

Still, on that evening we actually believed that Stourton and his servants had disappeared from our lives forever, thanks to Longspee. But, as we were soon to find out, even Ella had a thing or two to learn about ghosts.

9

THE STOLEN HEART

Both Ella and I decided that it was best not to tell Zelda or Ella's parents about our adventure. Had we told them, I would have understood completely if they'd banned her from ever seeing me again.

"We'll tell them when we're eighteen!" Ella whispered after the movie. "And they definitely won't believe us."

Edward Popplewell walked Ella back to Zelda's house.

The path across the dark sheep meadows is already quite creepy on a normal evening, and on that evening I was sure Ella was particularly grateful for the company, even if Edward explained Salisbury's medieval irrigation systems to her along the way.

As I crawled into bed, I missed Angus's sleepy hums and Stu's sighing the name of some girl above me, but rarely had a night been sweeter. My fear was still like a fresh scar, but for the first time in days I was again sure I'd be alive to see my twelfth birthday. I went to the window anyway, just to make sure there were no bloodless faces staring up at me. I gave a start when I saw something move by the garbage cans, but it was just Alma, who was taking out the trash.

It was a clear night and there were so many stars in the sky, it looked as if they were having fireworks up there to celebrate that Longspee had taken care of Stourton. I wondered where he was now. Back in the cathedral, waiting for another desperate boy to call for his help? I would have loved to have known more about his life and those things he needed to cleanse off his soul. I would have liked to repay him for what he'd done for me. But more than all of that, I just wanted to see him again.

And? What are you waiting for, Jon? I thought. *Go to him. This is the night to say thank you. You'll probably never feel as brave as this again.*

No sooner thought than done.

I stuffed a few of Angus's cuddly toys beneath my duvet to make it look as if I were under it. Then I put my clothes back on and, carrying my shoes in my hand, I snuck past the Popplewells' door and down the stairs. Luckily, our wardens always left the key in the lock. I pulled it out, hoping I'd be back before anyone noticed anything.

This time around, the close stayed empty of people

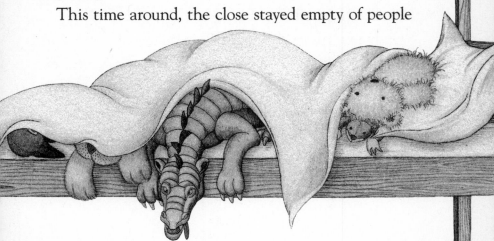

and ghosts as I ran across it toward the cathedral. The wall surrounding the cloisters is so high that not even an adult can climb over it. Fortunately, I found a tree with a big branch that reached over the wall, and I crossed it hand over hand. As I dropped onto the flagstones on the other side, I landed so hard that for a moment I thought I might've broken my ankle. But the pain quickly subsided, and the ghost of the mason's apprentice also stayed away. Nothing moved between the columns, and the moon painted silver patterns on the grass. The doors to the cathedral were, of course, locked and stayed shut, no matter how hard I pulled at them. What had I expected?

"Longspee?" I whispered, pressing my ear against the ancient wood.

A breeze drove through the branches of the cedar, but apart from that all was still. I sat down on the stones, my back against the locked doors, and stared at the lion on my hand. The mark had faded. Of course — it had served its purpose. I would never see Longspee again. I felt tears flooding my eyes. Great! Ever since I'd come to this place, I'd started crying more easily than my little sisters. I wiped my sleeve over my face and squeezed the lion mark.

"Why are you crying, Jon?"

I looked up.

Longspee was looking down at me. His tunic was still covered in blood.

"It's nothing. Absolutely nothing," I muttered, scrambling to my feet. I was so happy to see him. So insanely happy.

"That's what my sons always said when I caught them crying. Do not be ashamed of your tears. I have shed many in my lifetime, and there were still not enough."

The sword he'd rammed into Stourton's chest was hanging from his side.

"What?" He followed my eyes. "You look as if you've never seen a sword."

I had seen swords. Dozens. In movies and in museums. But I'd never seen one used in real combat. It had been terrible, even though those had been "only" the swords of ghosts. I couldn't take my eyes off the sword.

"It's probably quite heavy, isn't it?"

"Oh yes. I still remember how quickly my arms began to ache after my brother first handed me his sword. My fingers were too short to close around the hilt, and after my first training I couldn't even lift a spoon."

"Your brother? The Lionheart?"

"I had many brothers. More than any man would need, and all of them older than me. And stronger. They never grew tired of making the lives of their father's bastards miserable. But our stepmother protected us...the only one she'd let get away with anything was John."

His stepmother. Eleanor of Aquitaine. Bonapart had, of course, told us about her. And John was John Lackland, Prince John. The man who had hunted Robin Hood, if he'd really existed, which Bonapart denied most emphatically. I wanted to ask Longspee about his stepbrother, but he seemed lost in his memories. He looked down the dark cloisters as if he could see his brothers between the columns.

"Can I...may I hold your sword?"

Yes, I know. Very childish. (Though, if I'm honest, I'd probably ask him the same today.)

Longspee laughed. It wiped all the sadness off his face.

"No. Have you forgotten? This is the sword of a ghost. It is but a shadow, like me."

"But your ring!" I pointed at the mark on my hand.

"The seal remained with me. Death wants to make sure I fulfill the oath I took. All else, though, is nothing but shadow and darkness."

He looked at me. "Darkness taints my soul like soot, Jon. I wish I could once again have a soul like yours: young, untainted by rage, envy, and false ambitions. No more memories of bloody deeds to stay with me forever, no cruelty to shame me through eternity, no betrayal that took from me my trust in myself."

I dropped my head. Young and untainted? I thought of the gravestones I'd drawn for The Beard, and all the countless deaths I'd imagined for him.

Longspee laughed quietly, then went on in a

conspiratorial whisper. "What am I saying? Of course, you know of all these things. When I was your age, I wanted to kill at least two of my brothers. And I pushed my father's mistress down a staircase. Which earned me the worst beating of my life."

It felt good to hear his confession. But I still couldn't take my eyes off his sword.

"I still wish you could teach me," I mumbled.

"Teach you what?"

"Fighting."

He eyed me thoughtfully.

"Yes, when I was as young as you are now, I also wanted to learn nothing else. At your age I already knew quite a lot about it. I was not even seven when I became a squire." For a moment his shape blurred, as if he were fading into his memories.

"There's only one way for me to teach you something about fighting," he said finally. "I'm not sure whether it's the best way, and you may learn a few things you didn't want to know about."

"What way is that?" I asked.

Longspee looked at me as if he was unsure whether he wanted to show it to me.

"Jon Whitcroft *becomes* William Longspee," he finally answered, "for a few heartbeats...."

"How?" My voice was barely more than a whisper. There was nobody in the whole world I would rather have been, even though he was a dead man.

"Come closer!" he said.

I obeyed. I stepped so close that the light surrounding him made my skin look as pale as his, and his coldness seeped through my clothes.

"Closer, Jon!" he said.

It felt as if I were melting. I was in another body, even younger than mine, with a belt, a leather breastplate.... And there was another knight, as tall as Longspee, with a sword in his hand. He attacked me. I also had a sword, short and heavy. I yanked it up, but not nearly quickly enough. Pain. Blood trickled down my arm. A voice: *"Geoffrey! He is your brother!"*

"And?"

The pain was horrible. I could barely think. Where was I? Who was I?

I felt my body grow. Now I was strong and tall, but there was even more blood. And even more pain. There were swords, many swords, lances, knives, and horses. I fought. This time the sword was so long, I had to hold it with both hands. I felt my arms ram it into another body. I heard my own breath, labored and much, much too fast. I could feel rain on my face; it tasted salty. I smelled the ocean. I slipped in the mud and fell to the ground. Something dug into my leg. An arrow. I screamed with pain, or was it rage? There was blood in my eyes. Was it my own, or another man's?

"Jon!"

Somebody called my name, over and over.

"Jon!"

I felt cold and then warm again. I stumbled backward until my back made contact with a wall. I could still feel the arrow in my leg. My fingers felt for it, as if they had to convince themselves that it wasn't still there. My eyes, however, looked for Longspee.

He was barely visible. The light that usually surrounded him was gone. He was a shadow, nothing else.

"I was nearly killed in that battle." His voice seemed to come from far, far away. "There were many battles like that one, so many. And all that remains is the pain, the fear, and the noise. Fighting the French. Fighting my own countrymen. Fighting for my brothers, and fighting against my brothers..." Longspee's voice seemed to come out of the walls, from the tombstones that lined the cloisters, from the flagstones under my feet. "All that violence—whitewashed, because we were fighting for a just cause. Our cruelty was our holy weapon, as holy as the martyrs' bones we liked to wear around our necks. And now here I stand, covered in blood, bound by my own oath, caught between heaven and hell, and separated from the only one who could drive away this darkness."

I felt his sadness as painfully as I had just felt the arrow.

"What can I do?" I stammered. "Is there something I can do?"

Longspee's face was still all darkness. For the longest while he did not answer me. And when he did, it was not the answer I'd wanted to hear.

"Go home, Jon!" he said, his shadow melting into the walls of the cathedral. "Forget William Longspee. He is cursed. Cursed by his own oath and another man's deceit. He has lost his heart and the one he loves. And without her there can be no path out of this darkness."

And he was gone.

"No. Wait!" My voice echoed so loudly through the ancient hallways that it gave me a start. I listened in the night, and there was no guard, no priest. But also no dead knight.

I fell to my knees. It was the only thing I could think of. Ella would have been proud of me.

"Longspee!" I called. "William Longspee. Come back! A knight has to stay with his squire."

Nothing. Only a crow fluttered up from the old cedar tree, cawing noisily, probably complaining about the racket I was making.

Gone.

I knelt, feeling the sword in my hand, the mud under my feet, his heart in my chest. *Get up, Jon!* I told myself. *This time he's gone for good.* But just as I got to my feet, I heard a voice behind me.

"A dead man has no need for a squire, Jon Whitcroft."

"Oh yes!" I stammered. "Definitely."

"Yes? And what for?"

Go on, Jon, or he'll be gone again.

"To fulfill your oath," I spurted out. "To polish the marble on your tomb, to keep you company, to…to… find the path out of the darkness, and the one you love. Whatever! There must be something I can do."

He stayed silent and looked at me.

I thought he was never going to speak. But his outline had become clearer again.

"There is only one deed I could ask of you," he said finally, "and that is probably impossible."

"What is it?" I so wanted to do something for him.

I'd never wished for anything so desperately. I would've even bargained to keep The Beard in my life.

Longspee hesitated.

Then he said, "Do you dare to venture into my darkness once more?"

I nodded.

I stepped closer to him, until his coldness engulfed me again.

I was in the cathedral. At a funeral. Hundreds of people — men, women, children — were crowded between the columns. I could see priests, and choristers in the same blue gowns Angus wore. Candles and torches shone their trembling light onto Longspee's corpse. My corpse. I lay the same way his stone edifice did. A woman was standing next to me, very straight, and by her side were three boys and two girls. Ella. I felt how my lips wanted to say her name, but I no longer lived in this body. Everything was white. Everything was black. And suddenly I saw something else. A man was leaning over me. "*I heard you asked your wife to take your heart into safekeeping,"* he whispered into my dead ear. *"Very touching. Were you hoping she might keep you safe for eternity, our oh-so-wise Ela of Salisbury? Well, you thought wrong. I did not poison you just so she could stay faithful to you even after your death. No. Your wife will be holding my servant's heart. I had him culled just for that purpose. And he was such a good servant! Your heart has been put to rest between the old druid stones so that their poisonous shadows might kill your love as surely as my poison killed your body. You are forsaken, William Longspee. For I know well that you are nothing without your love. You will drown in your own guilt, and your soul will remain in the darkness, without any hope that your gallantry might yet cleanse it. You will not fulfill your fool-ish oath. Ela will wait in vain — here as well as in heaven. And your absurd loyalty will finally end."*

Willam's hatred choked me. I fought for breath. Such desperation! And I only became Jon Whitcroft again after Longspee had called me back a third time.

"Who was that?" I muttered, still feeling his rage as my own.

"My murderer," Longspee answered. "Find my heart, Jon. Find it and bury it at my wife's feet. Only that will give me the strength to fulfill my oath — and the hope that I may see her yet once more."

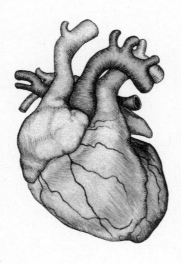

Poisonous Shadows

Alma must have heard something as I snuck back into the house. She came down the corridor just as I was getting out of my jeans, and I only just managed to shove Angus's stuffed animals out of the bed and to crawl under my duvet before she appeared in the doorway. Luckily, Alma noticed neither my wet jeans nor the muddy sneakers under my bed. She quietly pulled the door shut again, and I stifled a sigh of relief with my pillow.

That night I slept like a log, even though I had a horrible dream in which Stourton cut out my heart and buried it under a gallows. The next day I called Ella as soon as I woke up. She was with her parents, and her father didn't sound happy about a previously unheard-of boy calling his daughter on a Sunday morning. But in the end he put Ella on the phone. She listened in silence to my report, and she stayed quiet even after I had finished. I'd begun to believe her father had sent her back to her room, when she cleared her throat and asked me, in her usual *as if anything could ever shock me* voice, "And? What are you going to do?"

I'd really hoped she'd tell me. I'd so gotten used to her advice; it was no longer even embarrassing that it came from a girl (though it still confused me that she was so pretty). Ella was the best friend I'd ever had. And fighting demon hounds and murderous ghosts does tend to make you close.

"Jon?" she asked again. "What are you going to do?"

I stared at the telephone. At the other end of the corridor, Edward Popplewell was trying to put a nail

146

into the wall. "Well…" I finally answered in a low voice, "first I have to find those druid stones."

"Find them? What are you talking about? His heart's in *Stonehenge*, where else?"

Stonehenge. Of course. The most famous druid stones in the world. Even my youngest sister could draw you a picture of them. I was an idiot. A pitiful, dim-witted idiot. And Ella was again generous enough to pretend she hadn't noticed.

"I'll ask Zelda to take us there," she said. "My parents would ask too many questions. They are always so worried. Drives me crazy."

Their daughter had been nearly torn apart by demonic hounds and put to death by the poisonous breath of a dead murderer. I thought they had enough reasons to be worried. Of course, I didn't tell Ella that.

When I asked the Popplewells whether I could postpone my detention to the following Sunday, they retreated to consider my request. I'd told them the Littlejohns had invited me to Stonehenge. My house-parents deliberated for nearly half an hour before granting their consent. They really were great parent substitutes. I would have loved to have given Edward some stubble in return.

"Just be careful you don't get trampled by the tourists," he said when Ella came to pick me up. "Stonehenge is a dangerous place to visit on a Sunday."

Alma said nothing, but she gave Ella and me such a tearful *oh, such young love* look that I felt I had to quickly push Ella out the door.

Zelda's car looked older than the cathedral. Ella and I had to squeeze into the backseat because the passenger seat was taken up by a huge basket from which emanated some really strange sounds.

The road leading out of Salisbury was still Sunday-sleepy and empty, and despite her bandaged foot, Zelda drove so fast that every bend in the road pushed me against Ella, which was quite embarrassing.

"All right, then, I promised Ella not to ask any

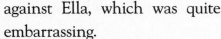

questions!" Zelda said, narrowly avoiding a cyclist who was struggling along the side of the road. "But I *will* say I think it's a little strange for your teachers to be filling your heads with stories about Stonehenge and hidden treasure."

Ella shot me a warning glance, and I did my best to keep a straight face while Zelda kept muttering about how much more qualified the teachers had been in her time.

Ella whispered to me, "I told her Bonapart claims there are mountains of Viking gold buried in Stonehenge. And we want to find it. Good treasure always gets Zelda going."

"What are you whispering?" Zelda asked over her shoulder. "Is there something I should know?"

"No! What would that be?" Ella answered with a perfectly innocent face. "Tell Jon about your plan."

"Ah, the plan!" Zelda smiled into the mirror. "Jon, you probably know that nobody's allowed near the stones because of all those druids who like to celebrate their rituals there?"

"Sure," I muttered, even though I had never heard of the druids or their rituals. But I definitely wasn't going to risk a long lecture about the history of Stonehenge.

"And to bypass that ban, we brought Wellington." Zelda pointed at the basket.

I gave Ella a puzzled look.

"Wellington is a dog," Ella explained with that stoic expression I'd already begun to find very reassuring. "A nice one," she added, as if all other dogs were like the ones we'd recently encountered. "He belongs to my friend Alyce, and he's really fast. Zelda will set him free to distract the guards, and we take the toad to the stones."

"The toad?" I repeated.

"Yes, there's one in the basket too," Ella replied. "Zelda says toads can find hidden treasure."

"By hopping around?"

"Exactly!" Ella said, tucking a trowel into her jacket.

This was, by a wide margin, the craziest plan I'd ever heard, but since this was all in aid of my finding a heart that had been buried more than eight hundred years ago, I decided I'd better keep my mouth shut.

It was cloudy again, and the wind tasted of early autumn, but that hadn't kept the tourists away. The parking lot was already filled with row after row of parked cars and buses, and the line of people shuffling past the stones on the other side of the road looked like a caravan of pilgrims paying homage to a strange shrine. When Zelda hobbled, basket in hand, toward the ticket booth, the crowd parted like a class of first graders in front of Bonapart. Who'd stop a skinny old lady with a bandaged foot? And nobody asked her about the contents of her basket either. (Nor did anybody notice the white snout that poked out from under the cloth Zelda had carefully draped over the basket.)

As we emerged from the tunnel that takes you from the parking lot to the stones, Ella's hair was attacked by a gust of wind, and my first glimpse of Stonehenge was through a web of black strands. Maybe that's why it looked as if the huge stones were performing some ancient dance.

"They're creepy, right?" Ella asked as we joined the procession moving past the stones.

I wasn't sure what they were. I tried hard to feel the poisonous shadows, but all I could see were some big gray stones that looked quite harmless compared to Stourton and his bloodless servants.

We'd circled the stones halfway when Zelda put down her basket and looked around at the guards who were keeping up a rather bored watch by the tunnel.

As soon as Zelda lifted the cloth, Wellington jumped out of the basket. It was probably no fun being stuck in a small basket with a toad. The dog dashed across the lawn surrounding the stones and performed a couple of perfect one-eighties before galloping toward the procession of slowly shuffling tourists.

"My dog! My dog!" Zelda shrieked so loudly that her voice would've been heard throughout a football stadium. The result was perfect chaos.

Wellington barked. The tourists stumbled against and over one another. The guards ran after Wellington...and Ella took the toad out of the basket

and sauntered toward the stones as calmly as if she'd come for a picnic. I did my best to follow her with an equally bored expression on my face.

It worked. Nobody took any notice of us.

Zelda was still screaming, and Wellington kept running back and forth over the trampled lawn. He was obviously having the time of his life. Ella knelt down in the shadow of the largest stone and let the toad jump out of the basket.

It made one uninterested hop and then stopped.

"Go on!" Ella hissed, prodding it with her finger. "Find!"

Nothing.

The smug beast just sat there, an expression of deepest loathing on its wide-mouthed face.

We tried near another stone. Nothing. Another half-hearted hop and the dumb toad again sat still, staring at the gray stones that reached toward the sky above it.

"What a flop," Ella said, giving the toad another nudge. The creature's only reaction was an annoyed croak.

I stared at the stones and tried to sense where the man I'd seen through Longspee's eyes might have dug into the soil and buried the urn that held the knight's heart. But all I saw was the road behind the stones, and the overcrowded parking lot.

Hubert de Burgh. Ella claimed he had to be the one, even though it hadn't been proved that he poisoned Longspee. But I knew better now. I'd heard it from his own mouth.

Ella put a comforting arm around my shoulder. At least I no longer blushed when she did that.

"Don't worry," she said. "We'll find that heart. You'll see."

I stared over her shoulder. One of the guards was standing behind her.

"Jon? Everything all right?" Ella asked, turning around.

"And what are you two doing here?" the guard asked.

His face was flushed. He'd probably been chasing Wellington. Seeing his huge belly, it really seemed amazing how he'd managed to sneak up on us like that.

Damned stones! They were so huge, even grown-ups could play hide-and-seek among them.

But Ella wasn't at all intimidated. On the contrary, she frowned and gave the man a look as if it were he, not we, who had trespassed. That frown is one of Ella's secret weapons. It immediately makes you feel like you just said or did something incredibly stupid, even if you have absolutely no idea what that something might've been.

"Did you catch my gran's dog?" she asked the guard, as if that was the only task that could possibly give some meaning to his otherwise pointless existence.

"No . . . no, we haven't," he answered, obviously quite impressed. "That's one fast little dog, that is."

"Well, then," Ella said, slipping the toad back into the basket, "I think Jon and I had better take care of it. If you'll excuse us."

With that, she strode past him as if she were the queen of England herself.

The look with which the guard followed her was so

puzzled, I wouldn't have been surprised if he'd done a curtsy.

We found Zelda surrounded by very agitated Russians, Chinese, and Canadians, who were all terribly concerned for the poor old lady who'd nearly lost her dog in Stonehenge. Somebody had even rustled up a chair for her. Wellington was panting on her lap, his tongue nearly hanging down to his paws, clearly enjoying all the attention.

"And? Did the toad find anything?" Zelda asked as she hobbled with us back to the car.

"No, it was quite a disappointment," Ella answered.

"Well, maybe there simply wasn't anything for it to find!" Zelda retorted tartly. She gently put Wellington into the basket with the toad. "Viking treasure, indeed!" she muttered contemptuously. "What nonsense. Your teacher will have to explain himself to me."

On the drive back to Salisbury, I was so quiet that Ella kept giving me concerned looks.

"Look, we can go back at night," she finally whispered. "There won't be any guards."

"And?" I whispered back. "Even if we dig around for a hundred years, our chances of finding that heart are one in a million."

Ella's look said, *Jon Whitcroft, pull yourself together.* But all I could think about was that I'd let Longspee down!

"Maybe it's by the stones in Aylesbury," Ella whispered. Up front, Zelda was trying to persuade Wellington to stay in the basket.

"Forget it, okay?" I hissed at her. "I'll find out myself. I was the one he asked to find his heart anyway."

I regretted those words as soon as they crossed my lips. But Ella had already turned her back toward me (at least as much as that was possible while belted in the backseat of a car). I think I never again got so close to losing her friendship.

"Who asked you? Are you still talking about your teacher?" Zelda asked.

"Yes, yes, exactly," I mumbled, staring out of the window.

Ella didn't look at me again, even when Zelda dropped

me off. And I couldn't think of a single word that would've gotten me back into her good graces.

No heart. And now Ella was mad at me as well.

All I wanted to do was to bury myself in my bed. But Stu and Angus had returned from their weekends. They'd brought back new supplies for the illegal candy stash, and Stu wanted to hear about only one thing: why Ella Littlejohn and I had been caught by a priest in the cathedral on Saturday morning.

"Why do you think?" I asked tetchily, throwing myself onto my bed. "We had a rendezvous with a ghost!"

After that Angus left me alone. He put a new fluffy dog next to his other stuffed animals. But Stu wouldn't let go so easily.

"Oh, come on. Ella Littlejohn? I'm *impressed*!" he said. "How did you manage to get her to meet you? And then she even gets herself locked in with you?" Under any other circumstances, the admiration in Stu's voice would have been flattering.

"Stu! Leave Jon alone!" Angus growled.

But Stu was on his favorite subject.

"Did you kiss her?" He had a new tattoo, a pierced heart, right on his neck. "Go on, tell me."

"For God's sake, leave me alone, Stu!" I barked at him. "Or I'll ask Angus to give you one of his special Scottish Hugs!"

I was in a miserable mood. I didn't have the faintest idea how I was going to find Longspee's heart, and I would've loved to cut out my tongue for what I'd said to Ella. I could still see her hurt face in front of me.

Stu, of course, took my mood as proof of something else.

"I knew it!" he said with a grin so broad that it barely fit on his scrawny face. "Nobody kisses Ella Littlejohn. Not a chance. I tried it myself."

"Me too," said Angus. He was stuffing his fluffy raven with gummy bears. "Big-time humiliation."

I admit that did improve my mood a bit. I pulled the blanket over my head to hide my silly-happy smile.

But Stu pulled the blanket off my face.

"Wait," he said. "We still don't know how you even got her to stay in the cathedral with you—at night!"

Yes, how, Jon?

"She . . . she wanted to find out whether there really are ghosts," I muttered. "For her grandmother." At least that was only a fifty percent lie.

"Yep, that sounds like Ella," Stu said with more than a hint of envy in his voice. Then he fell into a very unusual silence. He was probably picturing how it would be to be locked in the cathedral with Ella Littlejohn.

"And?" Angus was putting one of his T-shirts on his new fluffy dog.

"And what?" I asked.

"Are there ghosts in the cathedral?"

He'd obviously been asking himself the same question. "Of course not," I answered. "It's complete bull."

LONGSPEE'S CASTLE AND A
DEAD CHORISTER

When I got to school the next morning, I immediately went to look for Ella, but I couldn't find her anywhere. The old Bishop's Palace is such a maze of corridors and staircases that you can easily not run into a person for days, so initially I didn't think anything of it. During the first break Bonapart gathered us all for a bus excursion to Old Sarum to "give you an impression of how hard the

life of your Anglo-Saxon forebears was on that hill, which has no water and enough wind to peel the skin off your faces."

Great. But to me Old Sarum was interesting for another reason. I knew from Ella that Longspee had died there.

Old Sarum is a strange place. Bonapart clambered all over the sparse wall remnants and told us that the rubble to our left had once been a cathedral and that the pile to our right was formerly a palace. But all I could see were trees, bent by the constant wind, and a bare hillock on which tourists wandered among crumbled walls. And all the time I thought of Ella. We'd never fought before. It felt horrible.

As we climbed the steps that supposedly had once led to the royal palace, I asked Bonapart about the room in which William Longspee had died. But he only raised one eyebrow (he always did that when he didn't know the answer to a question) and launched into a speech about the military failings of Longspee, especially as the commander of the English right flank during the Battle of Bouvines. I pretended to be listening, but I let my eyes wander over the hills, the same hills Longspee's eyes had seen, and I wondered

whether Bonapart was talking about the battle I'd experienced in William's body.

Eventually we walked back to the bus, and the wind attacked us as if all the vanished inhabitants of Old Sarum had ganged up to drive us from their hill. Bonapart walked in front of me, desperately trying to brush his sparse hair back down over his balding scalp.

"Erm, Mr. Bo—uh, Mr. Rifkin?" I said, trying to keep pace with his hectic steps. "Do you know anything about Longspee's murderer, Hubert ... erm ..."

"Hubert Erm?" he repeated contemptuously. "Hubert *de Burgh*, regent of England, second-most powerful man after Prince John? Yes, I do indeed know a lot about him. And there is no proof that he poisoned Longspee."

"It was definitely him," I retorted. "But that's not what I want to know about. Did you ever hear anything about him stealing Longspee's heart?"

Bonapart gave one of his little arrogant laughs. "William Longspee's heart was buried in Lacock Abbey by Ela of Salisbury," he said. "In a silver urn bearing the

168

crest of Salisbury. Trust me, Whitcroft, Hubert de Burgh had far more important things to do than to steal the heart of a second-rate illegitimate son of the king."

I would've loved to tell him what I'd heard from Hubert de Burgh's own mouth, but instead I just mumbled, "Thanks, Mr. Rifkin. Very interesting," and wished that the wind would blow the last hairs off his arrogant skull for what he'd said about William. I was annoyed with myself for asking Bonapart in the first place. But who else could tell me about the heart?

After we got back to school, I immediately resumed my search for Ella. But then I heard from one of the girls in her class that she hadn't come to school that day. I have absolutely no idea what drove me to the school chapel after that. I don't believe in angels you call on in emergencies, nor in saints who have nothing better to do than to help eleven-year-olds with their history tests and other problems. (Angus very firmly believed in saints and angels. Before every test he always turned to Saint Angus MacNisse.)

No, I think I only went there because I wanted to be

by myself for a while. The chapel is usually not the most crowded of places, and I had some thinking to do: about Ella, Longspee, and his stolen heart. I wasted no more thoughts on Stourton. Yes, I know, not very smart. I know that now.

I squeezed into one of the narrow wooden pews and stared at the colorful glass windows, racking my brain as to how I might still help Longspee and also make up with Ella.

The lion mark on my hand had become more distinct again. I told myself that was probably not going to last if I kept being such a useless squire. Then, suddenly, I heard something rustling behind my back.

At first I thought the boy standing in a pew two rows behind me was one of my fellow students. The old-fashioned clothes he was wearing should have immediately made me suspicious. Yet his face seemed familiar. I was positive I'd seen it somewhere before. And when I looked at him more closely, I felt the same shudder I'd felt when Stourton's servants had stood underneath my window. Once you've seen a ghost, you keep seeing more. I do believe they're everywhere. Maybe they're the reason we sometimes suddenly feel sad or angry. Maybe love, pain, and fear don't fade as quickly as walls and stones. Yes, people disappear, just like the palace and cathedral of Old Sarum. But what if everything they experienced lives on? Like a smell, or the shadow beneath a tree? Or a ghost...

By now I've seen a good dozen ghosts. You see them only if they want you to, and I guess to most of them I'm just not that interesting. This ghost, however — the one I suddenly saw behind me in the school chapel — had been waiting for me. Just for me. I knew it as soon as I saw him. And as he came toward me, I also remembered where I'd seen his face.

Hanging in the hallway by the school chapel is a painting of four choristers, all of them a little younger than I was then. I'd always thought that the second from the left had *evil* written all over his face. I wasn't wrong.

He stopped next to me, and I could see the pews behind him through his gown. I remember thinking,

Oh, great, not another ghost! But when he raised his pale hand and showed me the lion mark, there were no thoughts left in my head.

"Why did you call him?" His voice sounded hoarse, as if he didn't use it very often.

I got up and squeezed out of the pew. He was smaller than I was, and after my experiences with Stourton, I wasn't really afraid.

"Who are you talking about?" I asked, though of course I knew the answer. I thought to myself, *Jon, you're getting better at talking to ghosts.* My counterpart sneered. I could see through his face as through tattered cloth.

"Don't play stupid. I bet you my place in hell that he asked the same price of you that he asked of me. Am I right?"

He laughed. It sounded awful, and his face quite literally nearly dissolved into laughter.

"Let me through!" I said, pushing past him. But he immediately stood right in front of me again.

"And where are you trying to go? Admit it. He tried

to get you to find his heart too. Our Saint William!" His face became so contorted that it resembled that of a cat more than that of a boy. "I called on him to protect me from one of my teachers. I was tired of the constant beatings, and I had heard about the knight who sleeps in the cathedral and who has sworn to protect the weak and all that." He bared his teeth just as Stourton had done. "Oh, he did help me. He had my teacher kneeling in front of him, sobbing, and the man never touched me again. But then I had to go and find the knight's accursed heart. And when I found it, what did I get?"

Through his chest I saw the pews.

"He killed me!" the chorister hissed at me. "And he'll probably do the same to you."

Then he was gone.

And I was alone again, staring at the spot where he'd just been standing. *Liar!* I thought. *I hope Longspee skewers your black heart, just as he did with Stourton's.*

Around me everything seemed to whisper, *He killed me. Killed. Killed!*

No. No, it couldn't be true.

"Come back!" I called, looking around the empty chapel. "Come back, you filthy liar."

"Whitcroft?"

Mrs. Tinker, the school secretary, was standing in the chapel doorway. Everybody called her Tinkerbell, though she wasn't tiny at all. Quite the opposite. She barely fit behind her desk. But whenever you were unsure which classroom you were supposed to be in, or when you needed a bandage, you went to see Tinkerbell. She knew everything about the Bishop's Palace.

"Mrs. Tinker, do you know anything about the boys in the painting out there?" I asked.

Tinkerbell turned in the doorway and looked at the picture. "Oh, those. Of course," she said. "The one on the right became an operetta singer in London—he had quite a fine reputation. The second on the left is the chorister who fell out of the window. I always try to feel sympathy for him, but..."

"He fell out a window?"

"Yes. Broke his neck. Back then there was a rumor

that somebody had pushed him. But he was supposedly alone when it happened."

I felt as if the ground under my feet were ripping open.

"I was looking for you, Jon!" Tinkerbell continued. "Zelda Littlejohn called. She asked whether you had seen Ella. Which is a little strange, since Ella didn't even come to school today. But I promised I'd ask you."

"No," I muttered. In my mind I saw the chorister falling out a window. "No, I've been looking for her too."

Tinkerbell shrugged and turned toward the stairs. "Well, let's see whether her grandmother has meanwhile found out where she is."

Hard to believe, but my mind was still not sounding the alarm. It was far too busy trying to process what the dead chorister had told me.

"Maybe Ella is with her parents," I said, following Tinkerbell down the stairs. "Her grandmother doesn't really get along with them." Ella had told me that her mother and Zelda argued at least three times a week.

But Tinkerbell just shook her head. "No, her parents

176

are off on tour again this week. Somewhere in Scotland, as far as I know."

That was the moment when I finally realized.

Something had happened. Something terrible.

My heart began to race so fast that I became nauseated. I forgot about the dead chorister and what he'd said about Longspee.

Could it be that William really was a murderer?

I suddenly no longer cared.

In my head there was only room for one question:

Where was Ella?

ELLA'S UNCLE

I ran all the way to Zelda's house. I didn't care whether I was expelled from school for playing truant a second time. I didn't care about anything. Where was Ella?

As I stumbled into the living room, Zelda was sitting on her sofa, surrounded by toads, a letter in her hand. She had taken off her glasses, and her eyes were red from crying.

"What is it?" My mind pictured Ella run over by a truck or drowned in the millpond.

Zelda held the letter toward me. The handwriting looked strange and clumsy, as if someone who usually writes with the right hand had used the left.

At first I didn't understand a word of what I was reading, but when the meaning slowly dawned on me, I had to sit down right where I was, on Zelda's carpet. My knees just gave in (and I nearly squashed two toads).

Zelda Littlejohn: Bring the Hartgill boy to the Kilmington cemetery at nightfall or your granddaughter will be in hell by sunrise.

Underneath the words was a sketch of a coat of arms. It was smudged, as if a clumsy finger had touched the wet ink, but I still recognized it. I had last seen it on a dead horse's blanket.

"But that's...impossible!" I stammered. "He's dead. I mean, for real this time. We saw it. Longspee killed him."

Zelda noisily blew her nose.

"Sir William Longspee? Jon, why didn't the two of you tell me about this? That's Lord Stourton's crest, but ghosts can't write letters."

Zelda looked at me accusingly, and she had every right.

So I told her everything. How Ella had gone into the cathedral with me on Friday night, how we'd called Longspee, and how he'd rescued us from Stourton and his servants. I left out only the parts about the dead chorister and the stolen heart. I just couldn't get myself to call Longspee a murderer.

Zelda listened. She was dumbfounded. When I got to the end of my story, she looked as if she'd like to kill me just as much as Stourton did.

"How could you not *tell* me about this, Jon?" she

181

hollered. "And what was Stonehenge about, then? We didn't go there for Viking treasure, did we?"

I dropped my head. I couldn't look her in the eye.

"That's a different story," I mumbled. "Really. It's got nothing to do with Stourton." I got back to my feet. "How could he kidnap Ella and write a letter, Zelda? He's a ghost. He can't even hold a pen."

"Holy stinkwort, how would I know?" Zelda said. "The ghosts I know don't hunt children or have demon hounds. They utter a few hollow groans and are gone as soon as you shout at them. What kind of mess did you get Ella into, Jon?"

She started sobbing into her soggy handkerchief again. I just stood there and stared at the letter still clutched in my hand.

Suddenly there was a knock at the door. I spun around as if Stourton had just poked his bony finger into my back. Zelda, however, dropped her handkerchief with a sigh of relief.

"Oh, good. That's my son," she snuffled. "I called him as soon as I got the letter. Come in, Matthew!"

she called, rubbing the back of her hand over her teary eyes.

"I really hope this is urgent, Zelda!" I heard a voice behind me. "I was in the middle of performing a root canal when you called. So, what's happened to Ella?"

I turned around, and there he was.

The Beard.

I'm pretty positive I've never looked so stupid in my whole life, and I hope I never will again. At least The Beard didn't look particularly sharp either when he saw me standing in his mother's living room.

"Oh, Matthew, you still have that horrid beard!" Zelda said, struggling up from her sofa. "How often do I have to tell you that you look like an idiot with that on your face?"

"You *know* why I have it, Mother," The Beard said, trying to force a halfway-sensible expression onto his face. "Or do you think the scar just disappeared meanwhile?"

"What scar?" I muttered.

"Bah, just a little accident from when he was still helping me with my ghost tours." Zelda squeezed a hasty kiss onto The Beard's cheek. "Jon, you tell Matthew the whole horrible story. I need some coffee. I can't think straight anymore. I cried myself out of my last bit of sense."

She blew into her handkerchief once more and hobbled off, leaving me alone with The Beard.

For the longest while The Beard and I just looked at each other in uncomfortable silence. I couldn't *believe* he was Zelda's son. He didn't even seem to mind the toads, which I thought was particularly strange for a dentist.

"Well, if this isn't a surprise!" he finally managed to say. "So, Jon, what happened to my niece? Did you get her into some kind of mischief, as you like to do with your sisters?"

Ah! No more camouflage. Open war. I could handle that.

"Nothing would've happened to her if you hadn't made sure Mum sent me here!" I shouted at him. "Really smart, sending me into a city where there's a dead murderer waiting for me. Without Ella I would now be dead myself. But how could I know he'd come back to get *her* and not me?"

Of course, The Beard had no clue what I was talking about, but at least he was now looking gratifyingly worried.

"What are you saying? *Who* got Ella?"

I gave him the letter and told the whole story all over again. While I was talking, he caught some toads — maybe it calmed him — and I tried to get used to the idea that The Beard was Ella Littlejohn's uncle. I would've loved to ask her whether she hated him as much as I did. But Ella was gone, and I was as sick with worry as if I'd eaten three whole bowls of that hideous mushroom soup the school serves on Wednesdays.

Where had Stourton taken her?

Was she still alive, or had he already turned her into a ghost?

Could he do that?

Zelda came back with the coffee. I was just telling The Beard how Longspee had driven his sword through Stourton's chest. I admit, The Beard didn't ask one stupid question. In fact, he listened as quietly as if I were explaining which of my teeth hurt when I ate ice cream. When I finally stopped, he just gave me a nod, as if he listened to stories about murderous ghosts and dead knights every day.

"Sadly, it all makes perfect sense," he said, dropping into the threadbare armchair that was usually reserved for the toads. "Stourton grabbed Ella instead of Jon because she's not a boarder and therefore he could get to her more easily."

"But how could he kidnap a child and write a letter?" Zelda cried. "He's nothing but a shadow!" She tried to pour her coffee, but her hands were shaking so badly that The Beard took the pot from her.

"I've always told you, Mother, you have a far too positive notion of ghosts," he observed, also pouring a cup for himself. "How could he write the letter? First possibility: Our murderous ghost lord has scared a living man into capturing Ella and writing the letter. Second possibility..." He hesitated and shot me a quick glance.

"What?" I asked testily. "You think I'm not old enough for your 'second possibility'? I bet you've never been chased by a five-hundred-year-old killer or fought with his demon hounds."

This came out of my mouth in such an aggressive

tone that Zelda looked at me in surprise. She still believed I'd just met her son for the first time.

"The second possibility," The Beard continued, unfazed, "is that Stourton literally scared a man to death and has given one of his servants use of the body."

"Use of the body? Ghosts can *use* dead bodies?" My voice was now no more than a terrified croak.

Zelda put down her cup and sat bolt upright on the sofa.

"No, they can*not*!" she said very clearly. "Stop telling the boy such stories, Matthew. You know I think this is utter nonsense. These are fantasies. Superstitions. Nothing else. Stourton has probably frightened some poor farmer by riding out of his barn at night, and he scared the unfortunate fellow into writing the letter and catching Ella as she came out of school."

The Beard reached for his coffee (which he drank without sugar, of course!) and took a long sip.

"But...but I still don't understand why he...why Stourton's still here!" I stammered. "Longspee sent him to hell. I was there!"

The Beard's mouth stretched into a grim smile. "But you said Stourton left his skin behind?"

"Yeah, so?"

"Well, he's a peeler."

Zelda rolled her eyes, but The Beard was clearly on to a favorite subject. Only once before had I heard him speak with a similar passion—when he'd explained to my mother the effect lemonade has on children's teeth.

"In the Middle Ages," he continued, "there was a superstition that a man who was hanged could save himself from eternal damnation if he soaked the skin of an onion in his own blood and kept it under his

tongue while he was hanged. It was believed that this would give the ghost a protective skin, which would keep him out of hell and could grow back seven times. Hangmen were generally told to look under the tongues of condemned men, but Stourton was, of course, rich enough to bribe his executioner."

"Seven times?" I asked.

"Yes." The Beard nodded as if I'd asked him the number of his fillings. "We can only hope the skin you saw was already the seventh. How many servants did he have with him?"

"Four," I muttered.

"Did they also shed skins?"

I shook my head.

"Hmm." He tugged at his beard, as he always did when he was thinking. "If we're lucky, he only managed to bring back one of them. Supposedly you can call back a ghost if you offer him the body of a dead man. To bring back all four of his servants, Stourton would have had to kill four men. That wouldn't have gone unnoticed in a small village like Kilmington. On the other hand, if they immediately slipped into those bodies..."

"Oh, stop it, Matthew!" Zelda put her hand over his mouth. "You always went for these dark stories, even when you were barely Jon's age."

"But how does he know all these things about ghosts?" I asked her. "Since when do dentists know this stuff? Or did he lie to my mother, and he's really some kind of secret ghost hunter?"

"Your *mother*?" Zelda gave The Beard a baffled look. "What have you got to do with Jon's mother?"

"She's the woman I'm living with, Mother. Margaret Whitcroft. I introduced you to her. One of your toads jumped into her lap."

Zelda looked at me with wide eyes. "Then Jon here is the spoiled little...?"

The Beard didn't let her finish. "Never mind that." He turned to me. "Of course I'm a dentist!" he asserted in an offended voice (though my doubts had been meant more as a compliment). "But what do you expect, with a mother like Zelda? When I was your age, she took me on dozens of ghost tours. I even had to dress up and play a ghost! So I read everything I could find about ghosts, but, disappointingly, still haven't met one."

"Well, at least that's about to change tonight," Zelda observed drily.

The Beard didn't really seem to be looking forward to it, which didn't surprise me. I'd always taken him to be someone who was much more comfortable with books and teeth than he was with real life. I couldn't for the life of me imagine how he was going to help us against Stourton. But Zelda had probably been unable to think of anything else.

A dentist, an old woman, and a kid. Poor Ella!

The Beard had let the letter drop to the carpet, and a toad had settled on it. I nudged it away and read the letter once more.

"Why are we still sitting here? We should go to Kilmington right away!" I said. "Maybe we'll find Ella before it gets dark."

But Zelda shook her head. "I'm sure Stourton will only bring her to the cemetery at nightfall."

"But where is he keeping her?" My voice was trembling, which was pretty embarrassing in front of The Beard. But there was nothing I could do about it. I pictured Ella in some dark dungeon, guarded by one of those huge black hounds, and I wished once more that Longspee could have taught me how to handle his sword. I would have cut Stourton out of all his skins and sent him to hell for good.

"I still think he frightened some farmer into becoming his accomplice," Zelda said. "That means Ella is probably in his house. That's how Stourton did it with your ancestors, Jon. First he held them prisoner on a farm, and then..." She didn't finish the sentence.

"Then why don't we look for that house?" I exclaimed.

"How?" Zelda retorted. "By ringing every doorbell in Kilmington and asking, 'Excuse me, did you kidnap an eleven-year-old girl because you were frightened by a ghost?'"

"'Or murdered by one?'" The Beard added, which immediately earned him another stern look.

So we all sat in silence. It was terrible. I felt that I was abandoning Ella after getting her sucked in to this whole mess in the first place. And our fight was just making it all worse.

It was Zelda who finally broke the silence.

"Fine, Matthew," she said. "Jon is right. What are we still doing here? Let's go to Kilmington. I want my granddaughter back."

The Beard swallowed hard, but then he nodded and got to his feet.

"You'd better go back to school, Jon," he said. "They probably called your mother, and she'll be wondering where you are."

"Didn't you read the letter?" I barked at him. "They'll hand over Ella only if Zelda brings me to them. I'm coming with you."

Zelda gave her son a puzzled look.

"I'm coming," I repeated. "End of discussion."

Zelda looked at me and wiped a tear from her cheek.

"Thanks, Jon!" she muttered. "Now my glasses will get all fogged up again."

"But you *can't* take him with you!" The Beard protested. "His mother's going to kill me. It's too dangerous."

"Matthew!" Zelda snapped. "If Jon doesn't come with us, then whoever wrote that letter is going to kill our Ella."

The Beard had run out of arguments — even dumb ones.

"Maybe we should inform the police," he said feebly.

"The police don't believe in ghosts, Matthew," Zelda said. She hobbled to the cupboard in which she kept her car keys. "And the letter says we have to come alone."

"And what about his knight?" The Beard put on his jacket.

"Of course!" Zelda spun around and looked at me, her hope restored. "Jon! Why haven't you called Longspee yet?"

I didn't know where to look. "Because...because he may be a murderer as well." I'd finally managed to get it out. "And we'll have more than enough of those to deal with tonight already, don't you think?"

THE CHURCH OF THE HARTGILLS

The Kilmington cemetery lies at the end of a narrow, sleepy road that doesn't at all look as if it's frequented by deceased murderers. To the right of the graveyard stands the very house in which the Hartgills once lived. It has, of course, changed a bit over the past five hundred years, but what stopped us in our tracks was the FOR SALE sign by the front gate. I'm sure each one of us had the same thought: Either the owners must have grown tired of living next door to a cemetery that was haunted by a gang of dead killers, or — if The Beard's stories were correct — the owners were no longer alive. I decided not to think about the second possibility.

The cemetery is surrounded by a high hedge, and the gate was locked. The Beard and I climbed over it. Zelda tried, but in the end she had to accept our help, which she did with a very grim face. I think she still had a hard time accepting that she was seventy-five years old.

All was quiet on the other side of the hedge. So quiet that I thought I could hear my own heartbeat. But there was nothing peaceful about this stillness; it seemed to be filled with stifled sighs and silenced cries — as if the earth itself had preserved the memory of what had happened here so long ago. Among the gravestones stood a church, its walls as craggy as an old man's face, watching us through its dark windows like eyes.

"No need to look for Stourton's name here," Zelda said as I scanned the gravestones. Most of them were so weathered that they poked out of the short grass like bad teeth. "He was buried in Stourhead, the seat of the Stourtons. I've always asked myself why he doesn't do his haunting there. This cemetery isn't even where he committed the murder. This is where William Hartgill was saved by his son's bravery."

The Beard was also looking around. "Who knows. Maybe Stourton doesn't like all the tourists in Stourhead," he said.

The sky was already darkening, but the sun wasn't going to set for another hour or so. What if Ella's captors had already frightened her to death? My heart clenched like a fist.

"Ella?" I called. "Ella!"

Of course, there was no answer. *Just don't start crying now, Jon Whitcroft,* I ordered myself. *The Beard will take it as further evidence that you're a spoiled wimp, and Ella wouldn't like it either.* But it was futile; hot tears still shot into my eyes.

Luckily, Zelda distracted me.

"Come on, Jon," she said. "There's something I want to show you."

The church was locked, so The Beard picked the lock with a piece of wire.

He noticed my astonished look. "If you like checking out deserted haunted houses, this is a necessary skill," he said matter-of-factly.

I wondered whether my mother knew of this side to The Beard. I decided not to tell her about it. Those hidden talents would just make him even more exciting in her eyes.

The air behind the church doors smelled of wax and wilting flowers, and it was as cold as a ghost's breath.

"This way," Zelda said, waving me along the central aisle. We stopped a few steps from the altar.

"There they all lie," she said, pointing at the tombstones set into the floor in front of us. "Lots of Hartgills. The two murdered ones are probably also buried here. Did your mother never bring you here?"

I stared at the names chiseled into the floor and shook my head. "I don't think Mum even *knows* about this place," I mumbled. "She's not really into ancestry."

"That's true." The Beard gave a quiet laugh. "Quite

the opposite, in fact. Margaret makes fun of people who poke around in their family history."

The look he got from me was probably not very friendly. I still couldn't handle that he knew so much about my mother.

Zelda guided me to a window on our right.

"This window commemorates John and William Hartgill," she said. "One of their descendants commissioned it. It's beautiful, isn't it?"

I nodded. It was a strange feeling to find out I had ancestors who were pictured on lead glass and were buried under church floors. I wasn't sure whether that was something to be proud of, and yet I was. I suddenly saw them all standing in a long line behind me, all those Hartgills who'd passed their name on to my mother. They'd all once been as young as I. They'd loved their mothers, and maybe some of them even had to deal with their own Beard. I felt them in my bones and in my blood. I heard them like a choir of voices in my heart. There'd been so many—that thought was comforting and at the same time unsettling. Those

names on the flagstones made it very clear to me that
one day there would be a gravestone with my name
on it.

Zelda tore me out of my thoughts, and this time I
was deeply grateful to her.

"I think it's going to be dark soon," she said. "Matthew, you'd better hide between those trees by the gate. Jon and I will stay here in the church. Call my cell as soon as you see someone or something out there. As soon as we hear from you, we'll come out. Then we'll pretend as if we're exchanging Jon for Ella, and as soon as they let Ella go, we'll distract them so the kids can run into the church."

That didn't really sound like a very sophisticated plan, considering we'd have to deal with Stourton and at least one living man. (I was still hoping that Stourton's helper would be alive and not, as The Beard had predicted, a corpse-skin on one of Stourton's servants.) And we'd also not be safe in the church forever. However, I couldn't think of a better plan, and The Beard seemed to have no problem with the role he'd been assigned, so I decided to keep my thoughts to myself.

"Fine, that's how we'll do it," he said to Zelda. "I'd better take the rifle, Mother."

The rifle?

Zelda noticed my incredulous look. "As a boy, Matt

always shot at the foxes and the falcons that wanted to get his rabbits. He became quite a good shot. And he only ever lost one rabbit."

"Yes, I still dream of that fox," The Beard growled. For the first time I could see the boy he'd once been. But even in that image I couldn't erase the beard, which made him look quite strange.

"My marksmanship may be a little rusty," he continued, "but I'll try my best. But what am I going to shoot? Bullets don't really harm ghosts, do they?"

"Shoot the live one," Zelda replied with a grim face. "He kidnapped Ella."

The Beard swallowed. "I tell you again, Mum, there won't *be* any live ones. And I hope I'm right. I'll find it much easier to shoot at a corpse, though I doubt a barrel full of bullets will stop him."

Zelda didn't reply. She just muttered, "I swear by all my toads, whoever turns up in this cemetery will leave unharmed only if I get my granddaughter back—without a scratch on her."

Her hands were shaking as she pulled a handkerchief

from her coat pocket and started rubbing her fogged-up glasses. The Beard put an arm around her shoulder. Then he turned and walked toward the church door. He opened it, and we could see that Zelda had been right. It was already getting dark.

"Matthew, wait!" Zelda called after The Beard. "My crutches are in the car. Will you bring them to me before you go and hide? They might come in handy." A rifle and a couple of crutches. That didn't sound like a very effective set of weapons against Stourton. I looked at my hand. The mark of Longspee's lion was still very clear. I was sorely tempted to close my fist over it. But then I dropped my hand. I just couldn't shake the memory of the chorister. Maybe that was the darkness that haunted Longspee — that he himself was no better than the ones he'd protected me from. And maybe that was the reason he was still here. Maybe all ghosts were either murderers or their victims. Had my dad ever come back as a ghost? No.

Fear gives you gloomy thoughts. And those are not always the sharpest.

Whatever. Waiting empty-handed for Stourton was not a good feeling.

"You can have one of the crutches." Zelda must've read my thoughts. Maybe she was a witch after all.

She hugged me to herself as if she wanted to break my ribs.

"Thank you so much for coming with us," she said. "You are a true friend, and there's nothing more precious in life than that. Ella is really lucky to have you."

"It's okay," I muttered. "Ella would do the same for me."

"Yes, you're right about that. She definitely would. But still — thank you."

14

CORPSE-SKIN

We waited. To me, it felt like weeks, months, years. Zelda kept marching up and down in front of the altar while I sat in one of the pews, where maybe one of my ancestors had once sat. I asked myself whether Ella was still alive. In books and movies, heroes can always feel whether those they love are safe or not. Since that night in Kilmington, though, I don't believe in that stuff. I felt nothing. Absolutely nothing except fear and helpless rage. I missed Ella. I missed her as much as if Stourton had cut off one of my legs or arms. How could that be? I'd known her for barely more than a week, and she was, after all, still a girl.

My mother had once said to me, "We make our best friends in dark times because we always remember how they helped us out of the darkness." She was probably not talking about times in which she had been hunted by vengeful ghosts. But I think there are many kinds of darkness that every one of us has to go through, and those are the times when, in order not to get lost, you need someone like Ella.

When Zelda's cell phone rang, I jumped out of my pew so quickly that I slipped and landed with my knees on the name *Hartgill*. My hand trembled as I grabbed one of the crutches that The Beard had leaned against the baptismal font. I followed Zelda to the door, and I felt as if all the Hartgills were looking at us, hoping that we might succeed at what the silken rope had failed to do: finally rid them of Stourton and take revenge for the two murders that had begun everything. But I wasn't interested in any of that. I just wanted Ella back—without a scratch on her, as Zelda had said.

It was a cold night. Fog had gathered between the gravestones, white and damp, as though the dead were exhaling beneath the turf. Four men were waiting in the haze. It was immediately obvious that there was something wrong with them. They looked as if their skin didn't fit them, and their faces were as expressionless as rubber masks. The Beard had been right. Ghosts could wear corpses like clothes, and Stourton had supplied not one but all of his servants with such a new dress. My heart froze in my chest. I could barely breathe as I gripped Zelda's crutch more firmly. My eyes, however, were looking among the gravestones for one figure.

"Where's my granddaughter?" Zelda barked at the creatures who had once been men. What a way to end up—as a corpse-skin for a ghost.

Zelda's voice didn't tremble quite as much as my hands, but I was comforted and frightened to hear in her words the same fear I myself felt.

Stourton's minions didn't answer. Talking is probably not easy for a dead man. But one of them turned and dragged Ella out from behind a gravestone.

She looked terribly pale. Her eyes were wide with fear, but I also saw a good deal of anger in them. She held herself very upright, and when one of the corpses grabbed her long hair, she kicked him in the shin. Brave Ella.

"Let her go!" I screamed, waving my crutch. I wasn't

sure at all how much damage it would cause to someone who was already dead.

The one to Ella's left uttered a horrible laugh and
grabbed her hair again. When he spoke, it sounded as
if his tongue fit him as badly as his new clothes.

"Your girl stays here, Hartgill!" he slurred. "Until the
silken lord comes to get you. He's on his way now."

"We shouldn't wait for him!" Zelda hissed, but just
as she firmed her grip on her crutch, the pale rider,
who had filled my past days and nights with terror,
leaped over the cemetery gate. This time he was

surrounded by light. Unlike Longspee's, however, his light made the fog glow a filthy green, like mold on rotting bread.

His new skin made him look even more frightening. *Which of his seven skins is this?* I whispered in my head. Not that it mattered. I was pretty sure I wouldn't live to learn the answer.

His horse scraped over the gravestones as if trying to wake the dead beneath, but the silken lord kept his eyes firmly on me. They burned as though his dark soul itself were on fire.

"There you are, Hartgill!" he snarled. "What are you waiting for?" He spoke as he would to a servant or a stableboy. Yet I was still a knight's squire, even if that knight was a murderer himself.

"Not before you let Ella go!" I called, cursing the fear that made my voice so shrill.

Ella, however, had her own opinion on that matter.

"I'm not going anywhere, Jon Whitcroft!" she shouted. "What did you think I'd do? Drive home with

Zelda while these monsters chop off your head or do God-knows-what to you?"

Chop off my head...I swallowed. She really did have a way of pointing out the obvious.

"Ella!" Zelda called. "Do as Jon says. Come to me. It will be all right."

Ella hesitated, and before she could move, the servant behind her grabbed her again. Ella rammed her elbow into his chest, and just as the corpse lifted his hand to strike back, Stourton stopped him with a sharp hiss.

"Let her go! I only want the boy," he growled. "Not that I wouldn't get him anyway!" he added with a beastly smile.

He looked more dead than ever. His teeth in a lipless mouth were so rotten that it looked as if he'd looted them from one of the graves. His hair was no longer gray but white. It hung over his shoulders in such thin strands that it had the appearance of cobwebs rather than hair. His new skin was stretched tight over the bones, as though it had been sewn onto his body like a shroud. His men looked no better, but they obeyed him in their new bodies as blindly as they had as ghosts. No wonder — centuries of practice probably did make perfect.

Ella still hesitated, until Stourton's servant finally shoved her in our direction. With every step she took, her eyes asked us exactly what our plan was.

There's not much of a plan, Ella, I thought as I started walking toward Stourton, who already had his bony hand on the hilt of his sword. *His sword can't harm you, Jon!* I repeated with every teetering step. *He cannot touch you — don't forget that.*

I'd decided not to think about what the corpses might be able to do to me.

Ella and I passed each other between two children's graves, which really wasn't very encouraging. *Come on, Beard!* I thought as we walked past each other so close that I could have touched Ella's hand. I suddenly remembered in a panic my mother's constant complaints that The Beard was always late for everything.

A shot rang out right at that moment. The bullet hit one of the servants in the back and spun him around.

"Run, Ella!" I screamed, shoving her in Zelda's direction.

The next shot came from the shrubs by the gate, and I heard Stourton utter some very old and awful curses.

Don't look around, Jon! I ordered myself as Ella and I ran toward Zelda and the open church door. Zelda wielded her crutch like Zeus's thunderbolt, but I could already hear the hoofbeats behind me. They sounded ghostly light, which made them even more threatening. *Jon, don't look around!* I thought once more. *He can't do anything to you. He can't!* But at that very moment, I felt a hand on my neck—a cold but very strong hand. It threw me to the ground, and I saw an ugly face staring down at me. It had probably been quite handsome in life, but now it was all skewed and contorted with rage.

"You are going nowhere, Hartgill!" Stourton's servant grunted, placing a muddy boot on my chest.

I saw Ella standing frozen between the gravestones.

"Run, Ella!" I screamed. But she didn't move, and another of the corpses, a scrawny fellow with blond hair, grabbed her, while a third one stomped toward Zelda. She slammed her crutch onto his bald head, but he just uttered an irritated growl and pulled the "weapon" out of Zelda's hands as easily as if he were taking a rattle from a baby. Then he dragged Zelda toward his hideous master.

Stourton was sitting perfectly still on his horse, watching with an impassive face as his minions gathered his human quarry. I looked around for The Beard, and I spotted him spread-eagle between the graves, his rifle on the grass next to him. For a second I was actually worried about him, but Stourton didn't give me a chance to explore that surprising emotion.

"Take the children up the tower!" he ordered in what sounded like a bad copy of a real voice, hollow and toneless. Yet the sound I heard behind me was far more dreadful. Zelda was crying. She cursed through her sobs, but still her tears made it more than clear: We were lost. No rescue in sight. The end. Curtains.

"I will kill you, Stourton!" I screamed as two of his servants dragged me toward the church door. "I will destroy you, you maggoty swine!"

"And how are you going to do that, Hartgill?" Stourton replied as he calmly dismounted. "I'm already dead, or have you forgotten that? Not even your knightly friend can do me any harm now."

I looked across at Ella. She had pressed her lips firmly together, but there was still not a single tear in her eyes. I couldn't be so sure about the dryness of mine.

The door leading up into the tower was so low that the servant behind us nearly got stuck in it. He kept shoving his fists into my back as I followed Ella up the worn steps. Halfway up we came past the windowless room where, as I'd learned, William Hartgill had hidden from Stourton while his son rode all the way to London to get help. In vain. In the end Stourton had killed both of them. *Just like you, Jon*, I thought. *There won't be any revenge. And this time the curse of the*

Hartgills will also claim a Littlejohn. That thought was worse than the fear I had for myself.

"Jon!" Ella whispered as we neared the top of the tower. "Where's Longspee?"

Of course! She didn't know anything about the dead chorister and his story. Yes, where was he? I'd wanted to call him ever since Stourton had come jumping over the cemetery gate, but I could think of nothing but his darkness, and my fingers were frozen by the thought that I'd trusted a man who had killed a boy barely older than me.

"He pushed a chorister out a window!" I whispered to her. "He's a murderer too."

Ella shot me one of her *what kind of idiotic boy-stuff is this?* looks.

"Bull!" she whispered back. "Just call him. Now!"

Oh, where had she been? Every one of her words blew through my gloomy thoughts like a fresh wind.

We'd reached the low wooden door that led out to the tower roof. The servant pushed us through it.

Stourton followed. The night blackened his bleached limbs, and his face was so see-through that a gust of wind might extinguish him. Yet the living corpse next to him still ducked like a dog every time Stourton looked in the servant's direction.

"It's a pity, Hartgill, that I cannot dispatch you myself!" Stourton said, smoothing his transparent clothes. "But I'm not really one for wearing some dead peasant's corpse."

The dead man beside him made a step toward Ella.

I stood protectively in front of her, even though she tried to pull me back.

"You are such a miserable liar!" I stammered. (My trembling lips couldn't muster anything more impressive.) "Do you know what I think? That you never had the courage to kill someone yourself. You always had others do it for you!"

My fingers felt for Longspee's mark.

"Yes, I bet that's why you don't dare move on to hell!" I screamed. "Because you..." Ella grabbed my arm, but I was far too angry to stop. "Because you're a damn coward who can't even answer for a single murder."

Stourton's red eyes darkened. I could see his skeleton under the papery skin. He looked like a terrifyingly convincing Halloween costume.

"Really?" he whispered, taking a step toward me. Then he pressed his pale hand onto my heart.

I saw blood. All over my clothes. I was Stourton, and I was standing on a dark field. In front of me were two bound men. Their faces were covered in blood, but they were still alive. One of my servants dropped his cudgel as I held out my hand to him. He gave me a knife. The handle was smooth and cool, and the blade reflected the flames of a torch. I knew what I was going to do. And I was going to enjoy it. . . .

It was a terrible feeling. More terrible than anything I had ever felt.

But then the knife was gone. Everything was gone — the dark field, the men — and instead I saw Stourton's pale hand in front of my feet, hacked off right beneath the wrist.

"Forget what you saw, Jon!" Longspee said, planting himself in front of me. "Forget it, do you hear?"

His sword shimmered with Stourton's ghostly pale blood.

I felt Ella's hand reach for mine. She pulled me back until we felt the battlements of the tower against our backs. They barely reached to our shoulders, and I could sense the precipice behind them like ice on my neck.

"No, not you again, you oh-so-noble knight!" Stourton taunted him. He drew his sword. "Are you going to cut me out of another skin? Don't bother. You can't harm me, no matter how often you defeat me. You have the wrong name to send me to hell."

One of the servants who'd come up the tower with us stood by his master's side. Another one was guarding the door to the staircase, which was our only means of escape. The other two had stayed with Zelda and The Beard.

"The wrong name?" Longspee asked. "And what name would I need?"

Stourton laughed. A new hand grew from his wrist, its fingers unfolding like the leaves of some flesh-eating plant. The hand Longspee had hacked off wilted and crumbled onto the tower roof.

"What do you think, noble knight? I can still hear the old man screaming his curse just before he died. *A Hartgill shall send you to hell, Stourton. Only a Hartgill.* Instead, I've been sending *them* to hell for the past five hundred years. My revenge for the silk rope. And not one of them came back to fulfill the old man's curse. They are like lambs that trot blindly into the shambles and expire. The boy you are protecting so selflessly will follow that same path, right here, tonight."

His servant made a move to step toward me, but Longspee pointed his sword at him.

"You think that dead flesh can protect you?" he said. "I will skewer your black heart so thoroughly that you will be awaiting your master by the gates of hell."

The servant hesitated, his face twisted with fear.

"What are you waiting for?" Stourton barked at him. "Get those children and throw them over the battlements, or I will send you to hell myself!"

The lackey took a step toward us.

Longspee's sword was as fast as a flame, and the corpse fell like a burst sack, filling the air with an awful stench as his rotten soul dissolved into the night air. Longspee's figure glowed brightly, as though he were made of white fire.

The servant by the door turned to run, but Stourton thrust his sword into the corpse's back and then turned to Longspee. Stourton's face had lost all human features; his skin was hanging in tatters from his bones, the rage peeling the skin off his body.

"Jon! Run for the stairs!" Longspee commanded. He was still shielding Ella and me with his body.

Stourton's shape turned a grimy red. It looked as though all the blood he had spilled over the centuries was soaking into his limbs. William, however, shone as bright as the white heart of a flame, and I no longer cared what the chorister had told me. I just saw the light and was again Longspee's squire, no matter what he'd done, no matter what was keeping him in this world.

"Ella, run!" I screamed. "I'm staying with William!"

Of course, Ella didn't move. I tried to drag her to the stairs, but she was—and still is—stronger than me.

"Let me go!" she hissed. "Didn't you hear what Stourton said? *You* have to kill him, Jon. You're the Hartgill who will send him to hell."

"And?" I retorted breathlessly. Behind us Stourton was raising his sword. "Just how am I going to do that?"

I could see that, for once, Ella had no answer.

Stourton snarled like one of his hounds, showing us his rotten teeth. But his sword was lighter than Longspee's, and the knight parried his blow easily.

"What are you still doing here, Jon? Go!" he shouted at me, blocking another thrust from Stourton.

But we didn't move.

You *have to kill him, Jon.*

They fought for what seemed an eternity—two ghosts, one so dark and the other so bright. There was no more time, just these two men who could not die, and Ella and me. Finally Longspee drove Stourton against the battlements and plunged his sword through him. But the silken lord just shed one more pale skin and took the shape of another, bloody red skin over pale bones.

"I have many skins, noble knight," he taunted Longspee. "And all the blood I spilled only made them hardier. What about you? Return to your tomb before I slice off your noble shell and make you my slave in hell.

You are as pale as a ghost as you were as a man. Helpless bastard son. Powerless among such mighty brothers!"

He hacked at Longspee's shield with such force that William stumbled, and Stourton's blade pierced deep into the knight's gleaming shoulder. Light flooded out of the wound, like steaming blood, and I charged at the two combatants with an angry howl.

This time I didn't wait for Longspee's permission. I stepped straight into his light and immediately felt my flesh become his flesh. I became tall and strong. I gripped the hilt of the sword in my hand. I was Jon and I was William. I was Longspee and Hartgill. Man and boy, knight and squire, fearless and scared, young and nearly a thousand years old. I felt my heart beat in his chest; his memories became mine, and mine his. And when I opened my mouth, I heard Longspee's voice speak my words:

"Now I bear the right name, silken lord, and all your blood-soaked skins won't protect you from me. A Hartgill will send you to hell with William Longspee's sword."

Stourton raised his sword with a hoarse scream, but I could see the fear in his eyes, and I went on the attack—with Longspee's strength and my rage, with Longspee's arm and my love for him and for Ella.

Ella, who was still standing behind us and who neither ran nor hid.

Stourton parried my sword, but I drove him back, step-by-step, blow by blow. And finally I drove my broad blade into his chest, so deep that it struck the wall behind him. His skins wilted like the petals of some hideous flower, and his burning eyes glimmered and dimmed. But I struck yet one more blow, hacking his head off his bony neck, and I no longer knew whose rage possessed me. Was it just mine, or also Longspee's?

Ella's voice brought me back to my senses. She called my name—"Jon!"—and she called Longspee. And finally I dropped the sword and went down on my knees, shivering. Stourton's shape crumbled in front of me, skin after skin, destroyed by Longspee's light and by my name. And then I was a boy again, who was kneeling on the very same stones where once William

Hartgill had knelt, waiting for his son to come and rescue him from the man I'd just killed.

Ella wrapped her arms around me, and when I looked up, I saw Longspee leaning against the wall. He looked so much like a living man that it was hard for me to believe he'd been dead for centuries.

"Jon Whitcroft," he said, "I think you are no longer just a squire."

15

OVER

Ella and I peered through the church door. The two servants who were watching Zelda and The Beard kept looking uneasily at the tower. They had bound their prisoners to gravestones, and one of them was holding The Beard's rifle.

Unfortunately, Zelda called Ella's name as soon as she saw us. Tears of relief ran down her cheeks, and The Beard began to grin so broadly that his beat-up face looked as if it would split in half. Sadly, that meant

Stourton's servants also spotted us. They looked at us with shock; I wouldn't have been surprised if their corpses' eyeballs had fallen out.

"Stay in the church, Ella!" Zelda screamed. The Beard kicked and wriggled like a hooked fish as he tried to reach the servant who was holding the rifle, but he didn't have much success. I have to say, I found the effort quite admirable.

"What are you staring at? We sent your master to hell—for good this time," I yelled at the minions. "Maybe you can still catch up with him."

The first blast of shot hit the door, barely a hand's width from my face. Ella pulled me back before the next blast could take off my nose.

"Have you gone mad?" she hissed at me. "Leave those two to Longspee!"

Longspee. He'd come down the tower with us, but where was he now? I looked around and saw him standing in the aisle between the pews. He was facing the altar. Ella, keeping an eye on Stourton's minions, waved at me to go to him. Luckily, the servants were at quite a loss without their master and seemed uncertain as to what to do next.

"Where did he go?" Longspee was barely visible, as if the battle on the tower had cost him all his strength. "Where did he go, Jon? Is there a hell? Is that where I shall go once death catches up with me?"

I had no idea how to answer him. I could once more hear the chorister's voice echoing through the school chapel: *He killed me.*

"Out there," I said, "are still two of Stourton's servants. They have Ella's grandmother and Ella's...uncle. Can you help them?"

Of course he could. Longspee stepped through the walls of the old church as if the ancient stones had brought him forth. The Beard stared at him with the delight of a child seeing his first Christmas tree.

Stourton's servants didn't run, though their corpse-faces clearly showed they were tempted. They probably still expected their master to descend from the tower and come to their aid. One of them took a shot at Longspee, which really was quite stupid. The second grabbed a shovel that was leaning against one of the gravestones. That didn't make much sense either. Then they attacked Longspee. But their dead limbs were no match for my knight, and they soon wafted out of their stolen bodies and dissolved into the night air, like their master before them. Longspee pushed his sword back into its scabbard, and the whole cemetery seemed to breathe a sigh of relief. The silence between the graves was suddenly as clear as the air after a strong storm.

"What is it about you and knights, Jon?" my mother

used to ask me when, for five years when I was a kid, I would refuse to dress up as anything else for Halloween. Yes, what? Maybe they let us believe that all the evil in this world can be banished with a sword and armor.

Ella freed The Beard (she called him Uncle Matt), and I untied Zelda.

Longspee was still there, but he was already fading.

"Why did you not call me sooner, Jon Whitcroft?" he asked.

Then he was gone, without giving me a chance to answer his question.

LONGSPEE'S DARKNESS

That night Zelda insisted on making up a bed for me on her sofa. She sent The Beard to notify the Popplewells, even though he looked nearly as dead as Stourton's servants.

"Just tell them you picked Jon up from school and the two of you had so much fun that you forgot to call," she said, gently nudging him out the door.

"Fun? Do I look like I had fun?" The Beard groaned.

But he did manage to convince the Popplewells to let me stay two more nights with Zelda. Then he spent an hour on the phone with my mother, who had of course already called the Popplewells and set them on high alert. Life can get complicated when you can't just tell the truth. *Please excuse Jon Whitcroft's absence. He had to save his best friend's life and break an old family curse.* We would've all given a lot if Zelda could have just written that kind of note to the school.

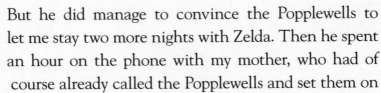

The next morning I woke up to a toad staring down at me from the sofa's armrest and to the sweet smell of pancakes.

"After a night like that, you can't just go to school!" Zelda announced as I stumbled into the kitchen. "I already called Mrs. Tinker and told her both of you have upset stomachs because Matthew let you have too many sweets. Luckily, she doesn't know he's a dentist."

The Beard was great for excuses. I was just mulling over how I could use him in the future, when he came hobbling into the kitchen. He looked much worse for wear, but that was not the reason I nearly didn't recognize him. The Beard no longer had a beard.

"I just felt so different this morning," he said, shoveling pancakes between his immaculate teeth. "The beard no longer felt right."

Ella gave him a kiss on his smooth cheek, but I wasn't sure whether I liked his face better this way, so I decided to keep thinking of him as The Beard for the time being (and I still do). But I had to admit, the scar on his chin was pretty impressive. Looking at it, I nearly regretted that Stourton hadn't left any such visible marks on my face.

After breakfast I finally told Ella about the dead chorister in the school chapel. She listened, as usual, with a deadpan face, which alone was enough to make me feel quite uneasy again.

"You have to tell Longspee about this!" she said. "I'm sure he'll explain everything."

"And then?" I replied. "He'll probably figure out that I didn't call him to Kilmington earlier because I believed the chorister's lies."

And that earned me a *Jon Whitcroft, you'll probably just have to deal with it* look.

"Fine!" I muttered. "Can you at least come with me when I talk to him?"

"Sure!" she said. "I still have to thank him for last night anyway."

Ella wanted to get locked overnight in the cathedral again, but Zelda crushed that plan with a particularly deep frown.

"Out of the question. No more nightly excursions for the both of you," Zelda said. "At least not without adult supervision." She'd managed to wangle keys to the courtyard and the side door of the cathedral from one of the guides.

"He's an old admirer of hers," The Beard whispered when Zelda proudly dropped the two keys on the kitchen table. "He supposedly etched her name into at least three pillars, and he never married because of her."

Ella tried to convince her grandmother to at least let us talk to Longspee alone, but Zelda shook her head so violently that her glasses slipped off her nose.

"Nonsense!" she said as we all squeezed into her car. "What if he really *is* a murderer? End of discussion! I promise I will only appear if you call for help."

We slipped in through the side door just after evensong. The cathedral felt like an old friend. Zelda went to wait by a column next to the font while Ella and I approached Longspee's tomb.

It seemed such a long time since I'd first come here. So much had happened since then. I felt like a different boy from the one who'd first called William Longspee for help.

What should I say? How could I look him in the eyes after having accused him of being a murderer? The murderer of a boy barely older than me.

I felt his presence even before I heard his voice.

"So, Jon...why did you call me only when it was nearly too late?"

He was standing between the columns, as if he'd been waiting for me.

I lowered my head. The chorister's words tasted like poison on my tongue. I loved William Longspee, but I'd seen the darkness in him, and the chorister had made me doubt that his light had always been stronger. Fighting Stourton on the church tower of Kilmington, I'd felt for myself how strong the darkness could be in all of us.

"I met the chorister. The one you asked to find your heart." I whispered the words, but the empty vastness of the cathedral made them loud and heavy.

"I understand."

There was so much weariness in his voice. And I could see the walls of the cathedral through his body, as if sadness and guilt had left hardly any of it behind. "What did he tell you?"

Telling him took more courage than fighting Stourton.

"That it was you who killed him. I know," I quickly added, "I shouldn't have believed him. It was probably not at all like that...."

"No, Jon. It's the truth."

I felt cold, as though I had Stourton's bony hand on my heart again. Longspee was barely visible in the shadows, but his words wrote themselves onto the darkness as if each and every one wanted to burn itself into my soul.

"But...w-why?" Ella came to stand by my side. It was the first time I ever heard her voice tremble.

William looked along the columns. "He told me he found my heart and he would give it to me under one condition: that I kill his teacher."

The knight went to his sarcophagus, where his effigy lay so peacefully in its marble sleep.

"The boy said, 'He's an old man,'" Longspee

continued in a very faint voice. "'His heart will probably stop if you just show yourself to him.' 'And why do you want him dead?' I asked. He laughed. 'Because I don't like him!' he answered. I'd heard that before, from a king. John always said such things. 'Get him out of my way. I don't like him.' And there was always someone who would carry out his wish. Sometimes that someone was me. I was tired of it. So tired. Tired of taking orders from a spoiled boy."

Longspee reached out to touch the stone face that looked so much like him. His fingers sank into the marble as though it were as insubstantial as he.

"I told him I would not fulfill his wish, and I asked for my heart. He laughed at me. 'No, in that case I'll bury it again,' he said. 'I hope it will make you so weak and miserable that you can never fulfill your oath. And you will never see your wife again. What would she do with a heartless knight anyway?'"

Longspee rubbed his face.

"In my helpless rage, I drew my sword. He stumbled

and fell backward out the window. He broke his neck. His cry etched *murderer* on my forehead, and that darkness tainted my soul forever. 'Just one more, William,' I told myself. 'It was just one more. You killed so many, and this one was probably bad.' But the darkness would not leave me, and I lost all hope of ever washing it off my soul. Or of seeing Ella again. William Longspee is nothing but a shadow. A heartless knight, bound to this world for eternity."

He dropped to his knees in front of his own grave and all the saints and sinners who were looking down at him with their stone faces. The walls of the cathedral seemed to be whispering words of comfort, and the columns stretched themselves as if they wanted to bear the knight's guilt with him. But the night poured its darkness through the windows, and the only light was that of Ella's flashlight.

Ella approached him cautiously, as though she thought he might send her away.

"You saved Jon and me," she said, "and Zelda and

Uncle Matt. As far as I'm concerned, your oath has been fulfilled, and you will see your wife again some-day. Because Jon and I will find your heart and bury it by her feet. I promise you that on my name. And now please get up!"

17

THE CHORISTERS' ISLAND

To his credit, The Beard did not ask any annoying questions when Ella and I told him that we'd need his help one more time. He appeared, as promised, just after the end of school and engaged the supervising teacher (Mrs. Bagenal, math and chemistry) in a discussion on dental hygiene so that Ella and I could sneak upstairs into the school chapel.

My idea had been to bully the filthy little black-mailer into telling us where the heart was, but Ella had frowned and asked how I was going to accomplish that. I, of course, had no idea, and so we did it her way. I hid between the pews (really uncomfortable!), and ten minutes later Ella sauntered in and looked around, pretending to make sure she really was alone. She's a great actress, as I learned that day.

"Aleister? Aleister Jindrich?" she asked into the silence. (Longspee had told us the chorister's name.) "Where are you? I have to talk to you."

She didn't have to wait long. Ella is very pretty, and Aleister's vanity was tickled that such a girl was calling for him.

At first he was barely a flicker by the altar steps. Then his head appeared, grinning like the Cheshire Cat, and finally the whole boy was standing in front of Ella. His chorister's gown looked like a bleached version of Angus's.

"Well, whom do we have here?" he purred, giving Ella such a sleazy smile that I would've liked to sock him for it. "Do we know each other? I don't think so."

Ella eyed him with a deadpan face, as though nothing was more normal than speaking to a dead chorister.

"My name is Ella Littlejohn," she said. "My grandmother Zelda does ghost tours in Salisbury. That's why I'm here."

"Indeed?" Aleister began to prowl around her like a cat around a milk jug. "Please do continue."

Ella folded her arms. The Beard had told us that supposedly stops ghosts from melting with you. He did know a few useful things, as long as he forgot that he was a dentist.

"I told my grandmother all about you," Ella said. "After all, everyone in this school knows about you. But Zelda says she can't talk about a boy who was childish enough to jump out a window because he was homesick and then found nothing better to do than to haunt his old school and feel sorry for himself."

Perfect. Aleister turned as white as a sheet. Not that he'd been very colorful to begin with, but it was a noticeable change.

"So, *that's* what your grandmother told you?" he hissed. He really did have a striking resemblance to a cat.

"Yes, that's what she said," Ella replied impassively. "But I recently heard a different story."

She paused for effect and smoothed her skirt. The girls' uniform is not very exciting, but Ella made even those clothes look terrific.

"A boy in my class," she continued, "told me that a knight who haunts the cathedral killed you because you stole his heart. Sounds much better than the homesickness story to me. But which one is true?"

"That's the truth! That blasted knight killed me!" Aleister stood on his toes to make himself as tall as Ella. Pompous little freak! It was no wonder neither heaven nor hell wanted him.

"Oh?" Ella brushed back her hair. "Prove it!"

"Prove it?" Aleister looked very confused. "How?"

"Show me the heart."

At first I thought he'd see right through Ella's ploy. But I'd underestimated his vanity. Not to mention that falling out a window and haunting an old school for centuries had probably done nothing to sharpen his mind.

"Fine," he said. "But if I show it to you, you will have to kiss me."

Little cockroach! I saw Ella swallow hard, her fists clenched under her folded arms, but her voice betrayed none of her disgust.

"Of course," she said calmly. "I always wanted to kiss you anyway. You look so good in that painting out there."

He swallowed it. Swallowed the bait like a dumb fish. Pathetic little blackmailer. Aleister had obviously forgotten that he couldn't touch people, even if they were as good-looking as Ella.

"I hid the heart in a safe place!" he whispered into Ella's ear. "It's not far from here."

So he *hadn't* taken it back to Stonehenge.

Ella masterfully hid her surprise. "Fine. Show it to me."

Aleister shook his head. "It has to be dark. My skin itches like crazy in daylight."

Ella looked at the colorful windows. "But that'll be

hours from now," she observed. "Why don't you just tell me where you hid it and I'll go and get it?"

Nice try, but not even Aleister was that stupid. His lecherous smile was back in a flash.

"No, I really have to show it to you myself, my pretty one," he purred. His voice sounded quite silly with its little echo. "Wait for me behind the school at nightfall."

"Fine." Ella actually managed an excited smile. "Just one more question: Aren't you afraid the knight might turn up here one day and ask for his heart back?"

Aleister's smile was so vicious that a stroke of lightning would've been the only appropriate answer for him, but apparently celestial justice doesn't work like that, even in a chapel.

"That poor dog can leave the cathedral only if someone calls for his help." He giggled. "It's got something to do with that silly oath of his."

"How stupid of him!" Ella looked at the filthy little creep, and her eyes betrayed her disgust, but in the next moment she was already giving Aleister her sweetest Ella smile again. "All right, then!" she said. "I'll see you after sunset."

The Beard hadn't had the best of times with Mrs. Bagenal. "Heavens, that teacher told me about every rotten tooth of every one of her colleagues!" he groaned when we met him in front of the school a little while later. And when we told him we had to be back at the school at nightfall, he wasn't very enthusiastic. He insisted on keeping us company until then, so we let him take us for ice cream on High Street. But when it got dark and we returned to the now-locked school gate, Ella made it very clear that she and I had to do the rest alone. Her uncle played the responsible pseudo-dad and tried to argue with us, but in the end he capitulated, since we were only meeting one ghost, who was nearly a head shorter than Ella.

In the moonlight the Bishop's Palace does not look at all like a school. As Ella and I scaled the wrought-iron gate, I imagined Aleister roaming the empty corridors at night, dreaming of the pranks he'd played on long-dead teachers and fellow students.

The meadow behind the school, where we always played rugby and football, looked, without its daytime throng of students, as alien as the moon.

"What are you still doing here?" Ella whispered when I stopped next to her in the middle of the lawn. "Hide, before he sees you."

I hated leaving her alone. The moon vanished behind a cloud, and the night suddenly became very dark. But Ella was right, of course. I found a hiding place in the bushes by the school, hoping that Aleister would take her to a place where I could follow them unnoticed.

Luckily, the little creep was far too keen to see Ella again to make her wait for him. She had paced the length of the lawn fewer than a dozen times, when the white figure appeared through the school's wall and started walking toward her. Yes, ghosts don't hover, they walk, and it looks very strange, because they do it a few inches above the ground.

I couldn't hear what the two talked about. All I saw was that Aleister's pale ghost body came far too close to Ella, and I would have loved to push him out a window all over again. As they walked off across the grass, I had a hard time keeping myself from jumping out of my hiding place and running after them. But I forced myself to stay, as we'd agreed, until it was clear where he was leading Ella.

That *where* became clear very quickly.

Aleister was heading to the island.

The name is a bit misleading. The island is nothing more than a little knoll that during rains becomes surrounded by water and mud from the little stream that runs through the school grounds. The first and second graders always go there to play pirates or shipwreck, and the third graders built a dam from branches and old crates so they could attack the first and second graders. After the rain of the previous weeks, that dam was the only access. As soon as Ella had crossed it, I crawled out of my hiding place.

I crept as quietly across the lawn as years of playing hide-and-seek with my sisters had taught me. Crossing the dam, however, was a near-impossible task. The branches cracked with every step, but Ella raised her voice to drown out the suspicious sounds, and finally I reached the island and saw Aleister's pale figure behind the bushes.

"I buried the urn by the stones over there," I heard him say. "It all looked quite different back then, but I'm sure that's the place."

Back then. Of course! After he fell to his death, he could never reach the heart again. That meant that it had been buried here for more than a hundred years, unless someone had found it meanwhile.

I peered through the bushes and saw Ella pull a trowel from her pocket — the same one she'd had at Stonehenge. She really thought of everything.

"What does the urn look like?" she asked.

"It's made of lead, with some magical symbols on the lid. But don't forget — it's mine!"

"Of course," Ella said. She began to dig.

Aleister stood right behind her. It was very hard to stay hidden while he ogled her with his ghost eyes, but I'd had to promise to show myself only once it was definite that the little creep had led her to the right place.

Don't you touch her, Aleister Jindrich! I thought. *Don't you dare.*

He can't touch her, you idiot! I answered myself. But that didn't really help.

"I can't see anything. Are you sure it was here?" Ella asked after a while.

"Yes, definitely. It must be there."

Ella pushed her trowel deeper into the damp earth. It felt like she was digging for hours, but finally I heard a faint *clink*. Metal on metal. Ella dropped the trowel and reached into the deep hole.

"I can feel it!" she called. "An urn, just as you said."

"You see?" Aleister was so proud; it made him glow in the dark like a white mushroom. As though it was a huge achievement to steal a dead man's heart. "So?" he purred. "Where's my kiss?"

Ella gave him an icy look.

"First I have to see the heart. What if whatever's down there is just an old cookie tin or something?"

Aleister's pale face became blotchy with rage. "It *is* the heart, and you will give me my kiss. Now!"

Ella got to her feet. She was still taller than he was, by far. "Really? And how's that going to happen? You're a ghost. And even if you were made of flesh and blood, I'd rather kiss all my grandmother's toads than you."

He tried to grab her, but his arms went right through her body. Ella attempted to push him away, which of course didn't have much effect either.

"Leave her alone, you dead little thief!" I screamed. I jumped out of the bushes so quickly that I stepped right into the freshly dug hole, twisting my ankle as I struggled to pull my foot out. But I still managed to stand protectively in front of Ella. The relieved look she gave me made the twisted ankle totally worth it.

"You get the heart," I said to her, keeping my eyes on Aleister. "I'll deal with the little creep."

Sounded great, but I didn't have the faintest idea how I was going to do that. Of course, I could have called Longspee. But how could I call myself his squire if I couldn't even handle a ghost who was five inches shorter than I?

Aleister had turned the color of a moldy orange. He was shaking with rage.

"What are *you* doing here?" he hissed at me. His eyes were turning into a pair of glowing embers. "Did that blasted knight send you?"

"And what if?" I replied. "It's still his heart, isn't it?"

"I will kill you!" Aleister screamed. His head was now glowing like a pumpkin on Halloween.

"Well, you can't!" I taunted him. "And believe me, I know what I'm talking about. I've had my fair share of dealings with your kind over the past few days!"

Behind me, Ella screamed with delight. "I've got it, Jon!" she cried.

She was holding an urn made of gray metal — lead, as Aleister had told her — and covered with symbols.

The sight made me forget all about Aleister. Ella shouted a warning, but it was too late. He had jumped me, and his body melted with mine, flooding my heart and my brain with all his rage and with so many images and sounds that I suddenly didn't even know my own name.

"Leave him!" I heard Ella scream.

I felt her arms wrap around me, making Aleister's iciness shrink away from her warmth.

"Jon!" she called, giving me my name back. "Jon!"

Aleister was gone as quickly as he'd invaded me. I knelt on the wet ground, shivering and feeling terribly stupid—and definitely not worthy of being a knight's squire.

"I should've known!" I muttered angrily. "I should've jumped to the side, or crossed my arms, or—"

"Forget about it!" Ella said, helping me back to my feet. "He sprang on me just like that as well. He's a filthy little creep, and I hope we never see him again."

The urn was still lying where she'd dropped it when she came to my aid. It looked like an old-fashioned flowerpot. Ella picked it up and wiped it with her sleeve. "Black magic!" she said as I looked at the symbols on its lid. "No worries, Zelda always tells me they

can only hurt you when you believe in them. Let's go
back to the gate. Uncle Matt's probably really anxious
already."

I'd completely forgotten about The Beard. As we ran
past the Bishop's Palace (and no, in the dark it really
doesn't look anything like a school), I thought I could
see an angry flicker behind one of the windows. In my
head I still heard the echoes of breaking glass and the

feeling of Aleister Jindrich falling through the cold winter air to his death.

To this day, I sometimes have one of the foul memories Aleister left like greasy fingerprints in my head.

Believe me, it's not a nice feeling.

18

EVENSONG

When we reached the gate, we saw The Beard prowling up and down behind it like a caged tiger.

"That took forever!" he cursed us. "What do you think your mothers are going to do to me if they find out that I waited here obediently while you two went to meet a ghost in the middle of the night? And don't give me your 'he was just a little one'!"

"Mum won't hear about this from *me*," I answered,

swinging my legs over the iron gate. "And it's only ten o'clock."

"Exactly," said Ella. She passed me the urn through the bars. "Relax, Uncle Matt. We had the whole thing totally under control."

Which was a big fat lie. But The Beard hadn't heard anything Ella had said anyway. He just had eyes for the urn.

"You . . . you got it?" he stammered.

I nodded and squeezed the urn tightly to my chest. It was all good, even though my head still felt gunked up by Aleister.

"We have to tell Longspee," I said to The Beard. "But you'd better not wait for us here. Aleister might still come after us."

Ella and I steered toward the cathedral. The Beard came after us. Of course.

I stopped.

"What are you doing? You can't come with us!" I really tried to sound nice. After all, he'd tried to save Ella's life in Kilmington, even if he hadn't really done much good.

"Yes? And why not?"

Because Longspee is mine, I wanted to answer. But of course I knew how childish that would sound.

His next argument didn't sound much better than mine. "I just want to see him!"

"Why? If you want to see a ghost, go back and look at Aleister."

"He's not a knight!" The Beard snapped. His face went so red I could see it even in the darkness. "I barely got a quick look at him in Kilmington."

"But if you come, he won't even show himself."

"Stop it!" Ella interrupted us impatiently. "It doesn't matter whether Uncle Matt comes or not. Longspee won't show himself anyway."

She pointed at the windows of the cathedral. Bright light flooded through them, and I remembered Angus telling me something about a concert for which the choristers had been rehearsing. I looked disappointedly at the urn, but Ella took my arm.

"Come on, we'll tell him everything anyway," she said. "He'll hear us somehow."

We snuck down the south aisle so that the practicing choristers wouldn't notice us. Ella and I were as silent as the stones around us, but The Beard couldn't keep his mouth shut.

"Just look at those columns!" he whispered. "Did you know they are bent because the tower is too heavy for them?"

"Yes, we know that," I whispered back. But that didn't shut him up.

"Do you know the story of how they found the place for the cathedral?" he whispered again.

"Yeah, sure," I whispered, squeezing the urn closer to my chest. Longspee's sarcophagus appeared behind the columns.

Ella gave me an encouraging nudge.

"Go on!" she whispered. "He'll definitely hear you."

The choristers sang as if a choir of angels had descended from heaven. It was always so hard to believe that Angus's mouth could produce such sounds.

Longspee's stone figure lay there peacefully, as if the boys had sung him to sleep. I went between the columns and leaned over the tomb.

"I hope you can hear me, William!" I whispered. "I think we found your heart. And tomorrow we will take it to Lacock, to your wife's grave. The urn is sealed, and that's why we couldn't open it, but—"

A loud voice interrupted me.

"Hey, Jon! What the heck are you doing here?"

I hadn't noticed that the choristers had stopped singing. They were spilling from the choir room like an excited flock of birds. And Angus was the tallest and loudest. When he called my name, all eyes fell on me, and I was standing there, the urn pressed to my chest, and I wished they'd all disappear to God-knows-where.

"Where have you been, Whitcroft?" Angus called, ignoring the disapproving look of the choirmaster. Like an excited puppy, he plowed through the rows of chairs toward me. "Stu and I were already—"

He stopped abruptly, seeing Ella standing behind me.

"Hey, that..." he stuttered, turning bright red. "Hi, Ella!"

She answered, "Hi!" and gave him such an icy look that I nearly felt pity for him. But Angus didn't even notice. He'd spotted the urn.

"What's that?"

"Nothing!" I answered, hiding the urn behind my back. And then...yes, I can't deny it, The Beard saved me.

"Hi, there!" he said, coming around one of the columns, holding out his hand to Angus. "Jon was with me these past couple days. I'm his soon-to-be step-father. I presume you're one of his roommates?"

"Oh, hello," Angus stammered, shooting me a nervous look. "Hi, Mr. Beard, I mean, Mr...."

"Littlejohn," the Beard said. Angus was probably racking his brain as to why I'd call someone The Beard who didn't have even a trace of hair on his chin. "I'm Ella's uncle, and I was just showing Ella and Jon my favorite tomb in the cathedral. This sarcophagus is one of the most impressive examples of medieval masonry."

"Yeah, Bona—I mean, Mr. Rifkin already explained that to us," Angus muttered. He was looking at Ella again.

The Beard continued to talk about medieval art and the tombs in the cathedral. He really tried his best, but I knew Angus was thinking of only one thing: that he would go back, shake Stu awake, and tell him he'd seen me with Ella Littlejohn again.

And, Jon Whitcroft, I thought while The Beard droned on, *what do you care what Angus tells Stu? You found Longspee's heart!* And yet I was still glad I'd be sleeping at Zelda's that night.

LACOCK ABBEY

Zelda wouldn't let us go to bed before we'd told her everything about the chorister and Longspee's heart. And she still sent us to school the next morning, but not without a solemn promise to look after the urn and to defend it with her crutches if need be.

School. Math, history, grammar. It all seemed so absurd compared to what we'd gone through in the past few days and nights. I wanted to climb on my desk and scream, *"Can't you see? I'm as good as grown up. In the body of a knight I fought a murderer on the top of a tower. I've become Longspee's squire, and I found his stolen heart! What do you think you can teach me?"*

But of course I stayed in my chair. During English, a rather hideous doodle landed on my desk, showing me and Ella kissing. All day I waited for Aleister to appear and demand the heart back. And he did appear in the end — in the boys' bathroom. But instead of the heart, he just talked about how confused he'd been since our encounter and how his head was buzzing with nothing but math homework and the strategic aspects of the Lionheart's Crusades. I was surprised our melting had had this effect on him, because school had been the last thing on my mind recently. But I was happy enough that he felt miserable, and I left him with the advice to just finally dissolve himself and disappear.

I did my homework in the backseat of Zelda's car. It was a long drive from Salisbury to Lacock, and this time the passenger seat belonged to the urn with William Longspee's heart. The seal had been broken.

"I thought I'd better check that it really contains what we were hoping for," Zelda had said when she noticed my look. "And I'd say the answer is yes. The content looks to me like what I imagine a thousand-year-old heart to look like. But, believe me, even if we were taking an old shoe to Lacock Abbey, the only thing that counts is that William Longspee now can believe in himself again. And that's thanks to you. And to his own courage."

The look Ella gave me made it quite clear she was glad we were *not* taking an old shoe to Lacock.

"Do you think Longspee will see his wife again?" she whispered while Zelda was cursing a truck driver who, in her opinion, was driving far too slowly. "Do you believe in heaven and hell and stuff, Jon?"

"I don't know," I whispered back. "But I really hope Stourton either dissolved into thin air or has gone to a place that will keep him away from me for eternity.

Angus believes in heaven. But I'm not sure. Problem is, if heaven exists, then who gets in?"

"Exactly!" Ella whispered. "For example, would Zelda get in?"

"I heard that, Ella Littlejohn!" Zelda said. She was overtaking the truck at such a hair-raising speed, I was afraid her poor old car would lose all four wheels in the effort. "And, no, they probably wouldn't let me in. But, anyway, I don't believe in a heaven or a hell."

Before I could ask her where she thought we go when we die, and whether her toads would go there too, Zelda was already steering her car into the parking lot of Lacock Abbey.

I don't think I'd mind if someone buried my heart in Lacock Abbey. You get the feeling the journey to the

next world is a little bit shorter from there, whatever that next world might be.

"I have a friend who works in the museum shop," Zelda said as she hobbled ahead across the parking lot. (She still steadfastly refused to use her crutches for anything but fighting ghosts.) "Margaret and I went to school together. She married an idiot, and she's not very bright herself, but she'll definitely help us."

Margaret was standing behind the cash register. She was quite tall and so big that you could've fit four Zeldas into her clothes. Her watery blue eyes bulged a little, giving her a look of being constantly surprised. Zelda asked after Margaret's grandchildren and counted the money for the entry tickets into her hand. But then Zelda quickly got to the point.

"Listen, Margaret!" she whispered across the counter. "I need your help. We have to bury something in Ela of Salisbury's grave."

Margaret's eyes nearly popped out of her head.

"What kind of silliness is this, Zelda?" she whispered back, shooting a worried glance at her colleague who was restocking the postcard display. "I've gotten used to the toads jumping around my feet every time I go to have tea with you, but that's really all you can ask."

"Heavens, Margaret, I haven't asked you for anything since I let you copy my homework at school," Zelda retorted under her breath. "So don't be like that. You do know the story that Ela of Salisbury buried her husband's heart here at Lacock, right?"

Margaret frowned. "Didn't she also bring her son's heart here as well? You know, the poor boy who was hacked to pieces near Jerusalem?"

Zelda shook her head impatiently. "No idea. The whole heart-burying fad was far too popular at some point. But, no, I'm only talking about her husband's heart." Zelda leaned over the counter. "Ela buried the wrong heart, Margaret. William Longspee's murderer stole his heart and palmed his servant's heart off to the wife."

Margaret squeezed a hand to her chest, as though she was afraid someone could do the same to her heart. "No! But that's terrible!"

"Relax!" Zelda whispered. "We have the right heart.

So show us where Ela is buried, and we'll set the whole affair to rest."

Margaret stared at the plastic bag in Ella's hand. "Is it in *there?*" she breathed.

Ella frowned and nodded.

Margaret gasped for air, and for a moment I really expected her eyes to drop out of her head.

"But, you see, there *is* no grave!" She exhaled. "There's only the memorial stone in the cloisters, and I'm not even sure Ela's actually buried beneath that."

Ella and I exchanged a worried look, but Zelda was not to be discouraged by such details.

"Doesn't matter," she muttered. "Then we'll bury the heart as close to that stone as we can. Don't you think Longspee might accept that, Jon?"

"Longspee?" Margaret's watery blue eyes zeroed in on me.

"William Longspee, Ela's husband," Zelda explained. "Oh, try not to look so obtuse, Margaret. Who do you think told us about the stolen heart if not Longspee's ghost?"

That did it. The poor woman lost it, and Zelda had to use all her persuasive powers to get Margaret to agree to come out from behind her counter and take us across to the abbey.

Lacock Abbey lies quite a bit away from the road, as if it's trying to hide itself from a world in which visitors no longer arrive on horseback, as they'd done in Ela's day. Margaret told us that the abbey hadn't seen any nuns since Henry VIII closed all the monasteries. I still felt as if I could see Longspee's wife behind every window, as though she'd spent all these centuries waiting for his heart.

"I think you're just trying to play tricks on me again, Zelda Littlejohn!" Margaret muttered in a low voice while we followed a tourist couple down the path that ends in the abbey's cloisters. "Just like when we were children and you tried to convince me there were fairies living in your garden."

"I admit, the story about the fairies was untrue," Zelda replied. "But everything else is the truth."

For a moment Margaret looked very disappointed, as

if she'd really hoped to one day maybe meet a fairy in Zelda's garden. But she quickly got over it.

She continued under her breath: "Two of the guards swear they've seen Ela of Salisbury's ghost in the cloisters!"

Ella and I exchanged a quick look, but Zelda seemed not at all surprised.

"Yes, I heard something like that too," she said.

"What? Why didn't you tell us anything about this?" I asked breathlessly.

"Because it's nothing but a myth, Jon Whitcroft," Zelda replied. "Do you have any idea how easily people believe they're seeing ghosts? Dozens have been sighted in this abbey alone, including Henry the Eighth and three of his wives, two of them, of course, carrying their own heads under their arms."

"But maybe..." I mumbled, "maybe Ella is waiting for William!"

"Waiting?" Margaret again stared at the plastic bag with the urn. "Heavens!"

Zelda looked at her crossly.

"Maybe," she said. "And maybe not. And maybe those guards just saw the ghost of some poor nun who died of the plague. A lot of women died in this abbey, not just Ela of Salisbury."

"But Longspee—" I began.

Ella quickly put her hand on my arm.

"Let's just find her grave, Jon," she said. And of course she was right—again.

But it was just as Margaret had said: Ela Longspee didn't have a grave. There was only a stone with her name on it in the cloisters. Ella and I stared, perplexed, at the stone-tiled floor surrounding it.

"Well!" Zelda said with a frown. "Probably can't do it right by the stone. However," she said with a glance at the lawn in the center of the cloisters, "Longspee might like it over there."

Margaret looked at her in alarm.

"Don't worry!" Zelda whispered to her. "We'll wait with the digging until the abbey is closed. What do you think? Where's the best place to hide so the guards won't spot us?"

The Littlejohns were obviously all partial to having themselves locked in at public places. Cathedrals, abbeys...I wondered where next.

Margaret, however, folded her enormous arms and shook her head. "Zelda!" she began, and quickly fell silent as a group of Russian tourists filed past us. As soon as the Russians had disappeared into one of the cubicles, she hissed at Zelda, "You're still behaving as if you could get away with doing things ten-year-olds do. You must remember what happened when you talked me into getting locked in the chemistry lab. It was *I* who got into all the trouble. No!"

"If that's the case," Zelda answered with a smile as sweet as marzipan, "then Jon will have to tell the ghost of Longspee that you were unwilling to help us. Just don't blame us if he comes for a visit one night. You've never met a ghost, have you? It can be...a little unsettling, and Longspee is not the most peaceful specimen — as Jon will confirm. But I'm sure you won't suffer much harm."

Margaret looked positively horrified.

"Well, you know," I muttered, "he's got a bit of a temper. And he has a sword."

Margaret pressed her lips tightly together. "Fine, Zelda!" she finally whispered. "But I'm only helping you because I've always admired Ela of Salisbury. It's just too terrible to think she might've been ghosting around here for all these centuries because someone gave her the wrong heart."

Zelda rolled her eyes over so much sentimentality. Ella really did take after her grandmother. Luckily, Margaret didn't see Zelda's reaction. She led us to a chamber that was barely more than a dark hole. Not even the most inquisitive of tourists would ever come in there.

"Are you sure I shouldn't take these youngsters with me, Zelda?" she asked before she left us. "I'd die of fear in here, even without any ghosts."

"No, thanks!" Ella answered for Zelda. "Jon and I've been in much worse places at night."

Margaret's look clearly expressed her doubts about Zelda's qualities as a grandmother. But Zelda just put her arm around Ella's and my shoulders and gave Margaret her broadest smile.

"Ella's right," she said. "These two already know much more about ghosts than I ever will!"

That statement finally sent Margaret back behind her shop counter.

As the sun set, our hiding place really did get as dark as a grave. But Lacock Abbey was ours as we crept back into the cloisters with our flashlights. No tourists, no guides, not a living soul with the exception of a few mice and birds (and spiders, as Ella would now point out; Ella's even more afraid of spiders than dogs).

We reached the gravestone, and Zelda said, "Great.

Time to get to work. I think this is something the two of you should probably do alone." She took a trowel from her pocket and handed it to me. Littlejohns obviously always carry trowels and flashlights. "I'll take a walk in the gardens meanwhile. I bet the only ghosts here are nuns, and those are usually quite peaceful souls."

With that, she hobbled off. Ella and I stepped over the low wall that separates the cloisters from the grassy courtyard. The rain had softened the ground, but it still took me quite a while until I'd dug a hole that was deep enough.

"Here it is, Ella Longspee!" Ella whispered as she

placed the urn into the hole. "I'm very sorry you had to wait so long for the right heart."

We did our best to replace the turf exactly as we'd found it. Then we scooped the leftover earth into the plastic bag and finally climbed back over the wall into the cloisters. The moon hung above the abbey like a silver coin. We were back among the pillars when Ella suddenly took my hand.

A woman was standing across the courtyard. The pillars on the other side of her were clearly visible through her body, as though they were part of her.

"Jon, that's *her*!" Ella whispered. "You see? She waited. She knew she had the wrong heart!"

"How do you know that's William's Ella?" I whispered back. "You heard what Zelda said. It could be just some nun."

By then I'd gotten so used to seeing ghosts that the white figure was no weirder than the pigeons snoozing on the roof of the abbey.

"Of *course* it's her!" Ella hissed impatiently. "Call Longspee if you don't believe me. Go on!"

Ella can be very convincing, but I still hesitated. I didn't want Longspee to appear only to meet some strange woman, but when the woman started moving toward where we'd just buried the heart, I squeezed my fingers against the lion mark. Then Ella and I quickly hid behind one of the columns and waited.

William appeared exactly where we'd buried the urn. His figure projected itself into the night as though the moon had brought him along. The pale figure of the woman stopped. They both just stood there, pale shadows of the humans they'd once been. Neither had been young when they died. Ella was the ghost of an old woman, but when she and William looked at each other, they became young again, the moonlight washing the centuries off their faces.

Longspee reached out, and when Ella did the same, their hands melted together.

My heart beat wildly, as if it was Longspee's heart again, and suddenly he looked around and peered toward where we were hiding behind a column.

Ella gave me a gentle shove, and I stumbled out into

the moonlight.

I'll never forget the way Longspee looked at me.

He pressed his fist to where his heart had once beaten, and I did the same. I'm sure I looked like a total idiot, but I think we all do when we're really happy. Except for Longspee. He just looked fabulous being happy.

I couldn't take my eyes off him, but Ella grabbed my arm to pull me away. I looked around once more and saw William's whole shape melt into that of the woman, and I didn't know whether I felt like crying or laughing.

We found Zelda on a bench in front of the abbey. She looked around when she heard our steps behind her.

"And?" she asked.

"All's well!" Ella said, pouring out the soil I'd dug to make space for Longspee's heart. "It was William's Ella, so Jon called him."

"Well, then we might as well call this a happy ending!" Zelda said. But when she saw how longingly I still stared at the abbey, she got to her feet and put her tiny bony hand on my shoulder. I think Zelda must have been a bird in a previous life, a very small bird.

"You don't like this ending very much, do you, Jon?" she asked quietly.

I felt so stupid.

"Well, I . . . you know . . . what happens now?" I stammered. "I mean, will he . . . ?"

"Go with her?" Zelda completed my question. "And, if the answer's yes, where to? Who knows? I never understood why some ghosts just disappear and others stay. Maybe I'll find out when I become a ghost myself—which, I hope, won't happen!" She linked her arm with Ella's. "I'd much prefer just being dead.

And now I've got to go to bed. This foot is still killing me. I might have to chop it off after all!"

And that was it.

Ella and I didn't speak a word on the drive back, but it felt good to have her sitting next to me.

FRIENDS

I t was past ten when Zelda dropped me off at the Popplewells'.

"See you tomorrow," Ella said, but I just managed a tired nod. Yes, I know, I should've been happy, but as I climbed out of the car and looked at the cathedral, knowing that I would no longer find Longspee there, my heart weighed heavier than a lump of lead.

Zelda had offered to let me stay at her house for the

night, but I felt it was time to return to Angus and Stu, and Zelda had let the Popplewells know that I would be very late — again.

Alma looked quite grumpy when she opened the door.

"Jon!" she said, leading me up the stairs. "I simply cannot let things go on like this. I'm glad you're such good friends with the Littlejohns and all, but you're still a boarder, and—"

"It will not happen again, Mrs. Popplewell!" I interrupted her. "Definitely not."

I crept into my room so quietly, I could barely even hear myself, but just as I pulled the duvet up to my chin, a beam of light shone straight at my face. Stu was looking down at me over the edge of his bunk.

"And?" he asked. "Where were you this time? Angus says Ella must've given you one of her grandmother's love potions. But I bet him my entire sweets stash that there's something else going on. You have a choice: You can tell us what's going on, or Angus will tickle it out of you. You know he's good at that, even though he sings like an innocent angel."

"I what?" said Angus.

But he didn't have to prove his interrogation skills. I told them everything. About Stourton, Longspee, his heart, the dead chorister, and Lacock. I'd had no idea how much I wanted to tell my friends everything until I finally did.

While I told my story, Stu switched his flashlight on and off like a lighthouse, and Angus muttered an endless stream of *wows* and *incredibles*. But they believed me.

"There you go, Angus," Stu said as soon as I'd finished. "Love potion, my foot! Your stuffed bird is mine!"

"What?! Your bet was that Ella's uncle is a contract killer!"

"And? He's a ghost hunter. Same thing."

"No," I said. "He's actually a dentist, Stu."

"Oh, really? And why did he shave his beard, then?"

Stu was not so easily defeated and was quite clear that he still thought his theory about the contract killer was much more exciting than a gang of murderous ghosts. Angus, however, stayed silent for quite a while. Finally he climbed out of his bed and picked up his pants from the floor.

"Okay, then. Let's go to the cathedral," he said, pulling his sweater over his head. "Maybe he's still there. I want to see him, even if it's the last thing I'll ever see."

"Angus! Longspee's gone!" I said.

But did I mention how stubborn Angus can be?

He wouldn't be talked out of it, neither by me nor Stu, who himself was not at all happy at the thought of traipsing around the cathedral in the dead of night.

When we found the downstairs door locked and the key not in it (something must have made the Popplewells suspicious), Angus suggested we climb through a window down on the girls' floor. Luckily, it wasn't too high, but just as I was crouching on the ledge, Stu of course had to tell me that Edward Popplewell slept with a loaded shotgun next to his bed and that half a year earlier he'd shot a cat off the roof, thinking it was a burglar. Angus said it was all bull, but I was still glad to see the Popplewells' window stay dark during our descent.

We got into the cathedral without any climbing. I had to swear a solemn oath to Angus never to tell how he got us inside, and I'll keep that promise. Being a chorister, Angus had spent many evenings in the cathedral, but neither Stu nor he had ever been there when it was dark and completely deserted except by the dead. The silence between the old walls was so complete; it seemed to come from the stones themselves. All we heard was the sound of our footsteps. The beam from Stu's flashlight etched a narrow path of light onto the flagstones. For a short moment I thought I could see the Gray Lady between the columns.

"It's this one, right?" Angus whispered, stopping in front of Longspee's sarcophagus.

I nodded. I was still sure Longspee was gone. Gone with Ella, to wherever one went after having spent centuries as a ghost. And for the thousandth time, I told myself that his leaving was okay, even though I already missed him so much that my heart felt quite sore.

"So, how do you call him?" Angus asked. Stu was looking at Longspee's stone effigy the way a rabbit might stare down the barrel of Edward Popplewell's shotgun.

"You call his name," I said. "And you say you need his help." I paused. "Please," I heard myself again. "Please, William Longspee. Help me!" It seemed years ago I'd said those words.

Angus and Stu stared down at Longspee's marble face — and didn't utter a word.

Then Angus mumbled, "He looks like he takes his oath quite seriously. Maybe he'll get mad if we call him and don't really need his help."

"Probably," Stu whispered. "I think we'd better go back. Alma always does her rounds before midnight. What if she sees that we're gone?"

She'll blame me, I thought. *Who else? Whitcroft, the night crawler.*

Angus looked at the other graves. "We could try calling someone else."

"I don't think that's a good idea," I said. "Stu's right. Let's just go back."

But Angus ignored me. "What about that one?" he asked, pointing at Cheney's tomb. As I said, Angus is very stubborn once he gets something stuck in that Scottish skull of his. And he'd decided he wanted to see a ghost that night.

"Bonapart told us about Cheney," Angus said. "He was the bodyguard of Edward the Something and the standard-bearer of Henry the Seventh."

Stu looked at me in alarm.

I tried to distract Angus. "Henry the Seventh? Wasn't he found dead in some bush?"

"No, that was Richard," he said, walking toward Cheney's sarcophagus. "They called Cheney *the Giant*," he mumbled reverently.

"The Giant?" Stu breathed. "Why?"

"Doctors measured the bones of his skeleton," Angus answered. "And they found he was at least six foot six. Quite tall for back then."

And it still is if you're Stu's height. "I don't think that sounds as if I want to meet him!" he said. He tried to pull Angus away from the sarcophagus. "Come on. If you have to call a ghost, let's find someone our size. Didn't Bonapart tell us about some child bishop who's buried here?"

But Angus shook him off. "No!" he said. "I don't want just any ghost. It's got to be a knight." He cleared his throat and put his hands on Cheney's marble chest. "Ahem. Hello. I mean, please, Sir Cheney…"

"He'll only come if you put some coins on his forehead," a voice behind us said.

Angus and Stu turned as white as Cheney's stone effigy. But I recognized that voice, and I felt dizzy with happiness.

Longspee was standing next to his tomb. He was glowing as brightly as if all the candles in the cathedral had lent him their light. I'd never seen him that clearly. And he looked happy. Just happy.

"You want them to see me, Jon. Am I right?" he

asked. Angus's and Stu's mouths were as wide as the gargoyles' outside.

"Yes, this is great!" I muttered. I'd been so sure I'd never see him again. My heart was drowning in happiness. "Longspee! Why are you still here?"

"You may not be the last to need my help," he answered.

"But what about Ella?"

"Now that you brought her my heart, she can call me anytime." Longspee turned to Angus and Stu. He smiled as they drew back from him. "If you're already afraid of me, lads, maybe you really shouldn't call Cheney," he said. "He can be quite rough."

Stu opened his mouth, but no sound came out.

Angus, however, handled himself quite well, considering it was the first time he'd spoken to a ghost. "Well, I haven't got any coins with me anyway," he muttered.

"There *is* another way to call this knight," Longspee said. "Are you sure?"

Stu quickly shook his head, but Angus nodded

vehemently, and Longspee went to stand by Cheney's tomb.

We all shrank back as he drew his sword. He stabbed it deep into Cheney's marble chest. From the tomb came a curse that would have earned us all at least a dozen weeks of detention in the school library.

"Damned be you, Longspee! You devious scoundrel of a knight!" The words echoed through the cathedral. For a moment it looked as if Cheney's marble effigy was rising. But it was just his ghost lifting himself out of the stone. He swung his legs from the stone pedestal and stalked stiffly toward Longspee. He towered over William by at least a head.

"What is it, royal bastard?" he growled, throwing back his long hair, which was as silver as the rest of him. "You feel like a little joust in the cloisters? If not, what did you wake me for?"

"Not tonight," Longspee answered. "I wanted to introduce the friends of my squire."

Cheney turned to face us. Stu inched even closer to Angus's side.

"Your *squire?*" he asked, scratching his huge neck. Even ghosts get itchy skin sometimes. "Which one is it?"

I raised my hand. "Me. Jon Whitcroft." I nearly added, "Hartgill on my mother's side," as I stepped to Longspee's side. But the ghost to whom that would have meant something was gone and forgotten.

Cheney eyed me from head to toe. Then he shoved his fist into Longspee's chest. "Does that mean you now have a squire and I don't?"

"*I* could be your squire...sir!" Angus stepped forward so eagerly that he stumbled over his own feet.

Cheney sneezed into his pale hand and gave Angus a disparaging look. "*You?* You look suspiciously like a Scot!" he snorted disdainfully. "Everybody knows Scots are far too troublesome to make good squires. On the other hand," he added with a look at Stu, "you're a good bit better than your scrawny friend. He wouldn't even make a good lance shaft!" Cheney started laughing.

"Very funny!" Stu replied in an injured voice. The insult had obviously made him forget his fear. "From what I heard from Jon, your kind can't even lift a feather, let alone a lance!"

"I think I have to teach you some respect, you scrawny little weasel!" Cheney growled, advancing toward Stu. But Longspee stepped into his path.

"Go back to sleep, John!" he said. "Your mood really is abominable when you are awoken before midnight."

In reply, Cheney yawned so thoroughly that we could see the whole cathedral through his mouth.

"Are you the only ghosts here?" Angus asked. He obviously still liked the knight, despite his comment about Scottish squires.

"No," Longspee answered. "This cathedral is home to many, but most show themselves only to their own kind."

"And then they spend most of their time moaning," Cheney observed. "I shall go back to sleep. I hope the next time I get woken up, it will be by someone who knows how to pay a knight." And he was gone.

Angus stared at Cheney's tomb as longingly as a dog would at his master's grave. I only had eyes for Longspee, whose shape was starting to fade.

"Wait, Longspee!" I called after him. "How will I see you again?"

"You are my squire, Jon Whitcroft," he answered. "You can call me anytime. And I, you."

That is true to this day. I've never made him wait, and neither has he.

Maybe the full moon made all the ghosts in the cathedral restless that night. We met the mason's apprentice in one of the cloisters. He wasn't much older than we were, but he was cloaked in so much misery that we could feel it like a cold shadow. Stu announced he'd had enough of ghosts for one night.

We didn't get to see Edward Popplewell's shotgun as we climbed back in through the window on the first floor, and to this day I'm not sure whether Stu made up that story. It was long after midnight, but none of us felt like sleeping, and so we played cards on Stu's bed by flashlight. I still think none of us wanted that night to end because we knew that the memory of all we'd seen would fade in the daylight, just like Longspee.

21

Not Such a Bad Place

Three days later Mum came to Salisbury, and that morning, as I brushed my teeth, I tried to put the grumpy expression I'd mastered so perfectly back on my face. But it just felt as if I were looking at Aleister Jindrich's eternally pouty face in the mirror.

"Yep, Jon Whitcroft, you might as well admit it," I whispered to my reflection, even though that earned me an irritated look from Stu, who was standing next to me, scrubbing away at one of his tattoos. "You're having a good time here, even though you were nearly torn to pieces by a pack of demon hounds and almost thrown off a church tower."

I had no intention of telling Mum about any of that.

She picked me up from school and took me to the café on Market Square, where the cake is so good that Stu sometimes groans about it in his sleep. She was as nervous as I was. I could see it in the way she clutched the straps of the horrible handbag The Beard had bought her as an engagement present. As promised, she'd come without him, but she couldn't spare me the kisses and hugs in front of Angus and Stu. The two of them also have mothers and, like true friends, they both pretended they hadn't seen anything. As Mum and I walked toward the school gate, I spotted Ella walking ahead of us with some of her friends. I didn't dare to call out to her. Her friends were terrible gossips—and still are. *Ella, I would like you to meet my mother* would've probably given them material for weeks of scandalous rumors. But I couldn't help staring after her. Her dark hair fell over her back as Ela of Salisbury's veil had back in Lacock.

"What is it?" Mum put her hand on my shoulder.

"Nothing," I mumbled. Ella walked out of sight between the trees at the end of the road. I'd already told her that Longspee hadn't disappeared from the cathedral, and I would've loved to walk with her across the sheep meadows to Zelda's house, talking about everything and nothing. Nobody did that as well as Ella.

"Nothing?" Mum asked. "I can see you're thinking about something."

Oh dear. This was going to get difficult. What should I talk to her about? School? Teachers? Talking to someone is really hard when you have to avoid all those topics that really matter to you. But I was still determined not to tell Mum anything about Stourton or Longspee.

"Jon?" *Uh-oh.* Her tone meant that things were

about to get serious. "I came here to talk to you about something."

"Mum!" I quickly interrupted her. "We don't have to talk. Really. We don't."

That plunged her into an awkward silence all the way up High Street, except for the short story she told about my youngest sister, who'd rescued a bird with a broken leg and brought it into the house.

The café on Market Square was quite full, so we climbed the stairs to the second floor, where the only other customers were three old ladies sipping their tea. They eyed us inquisitively as we sat down at one of the tables by the window. I was just biting into my second éclair when my mother cleared her throat. She had started making knots in her napkin (which, considering it was a paper napkin, was not a mean feat).

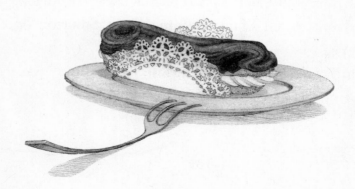

"Jon?" she said again. "I'm here to tell you that you can come home now."

I nearly choked on my Coke. I know. Terribly embarrassing. All that foam coming out of my nose, and my mum slapping my back in a panic. When I could finally breathe again, she told me proudly that she'd already spoken to the headmaster. I had won! I'd really won! But all I could think about was no more Ella, no more Angus, no more Stu. No more elderberry lemonade on Zelda's sofa, no more Alma-lavender-soap smell. No more Popplewells, no Bishop's Palace, no more chorister gowns swishing along the corridors, no more Tinkerbell greetings first thing in the morning ("*Hello,*

Jon, another glorious day today, isn't it?"). I was sure I'd even miss Bonapart, and even dead old Aleister, not to mention Longspee.

"...and be that as it may," I heard my mum say, "you will no doubt be glad to hear that I'm no longer sure whether Matthew is really the right man for me."

"*What?*" I stared at her so intently that her face became bright red.

"He...a few days ago he drove to his mother's. I've met her only once. She's a little unusual. I'm not sure... have I told you she has toads in her house? Anyway... Matthew went to see her on some urgent family business, and since he's been back, he's been acting very strange. He shaved off his beard, which is good, since I never really liked it, but he keeps asking the strangest questions. Whether I believe in ghosts and what I think about knights and whether"—she took a quick sip of her coffee—"and whether, after his death, I would bury his heart in our garden. I know you never liked him, and I should've asked you why. But anyway, I won't be marrying him after all."

She had tears in her eyes, and I knew she expected some expression of joy from me. But instead I just sat there, the éclair in my sticky fingers, and all I could think about was The Beard hiding himself in the bushes in the Kilmington cemetery with Zelda's rifle.

"I actually think that's not a good enough reason, Mum," I heard myself say. I could've bitten off my own tongue!

"What? What are you doing?" Mum was wiping her eyes with her napkin, smudging her makeup in the process. "Are you making fun of me, Jon?" she asked testily.

"No, I'm totally serious!" I whispered intently. (The three ladies were starting to lean in our direction.) "And those questions he asks...I think they're really good questions."

I had no idea what had come over me. Had Longspee brought out my noble side? *"You idiot! Here's your chance to get rid of The Beard for good!"* my not-so-noble self whispered. *"Take it!"* But my noble side whispered back rather cunningly, *"Really? Does that mean you'd like to get rid of Ella as well? He's her uncle, after all."*

My mother was staring at me in disbelief. "Really good questions?" she asked.

Wrong topic, Jon! Quickly, change the subject.

"Mum," I said, taking another fortifying bite of my éclair, though that didn't make talking any easier. "Actually...I don't really want to go home. I like it here. So why don't you marry The Beard, and I'll come visit every other weekend?"

"Oh, Jon!" she sobbed, and her tears started really flowing. They rolled freely down her face, and one of the old ladies came over to give her a handkerchief (quite a hideous one, with pink lace and embroidered roses). The look the woman gave me made it quite clear what she thought about children in general and me in particular. My mother, however, smudged her black eyeliner all over the printed roses and began to giggle. Now the looks from the three ladies also made it quite clear what they thought about giggling mothers.

"Mum!" I whispered across the table. "It's fine! I can come every weekend if you like."

"Oh, Jon!" she whispered back, rubbing her eyes with the handkerchief. Then she leaned across the table, pulled me close, whispered, "Thank you," and hugged me so hard that I thought she wasn't going to ever let go. But when she did, she looked very happy. She even gave the three ladies a smile. Then she returned the soggy, blackened handkerchief, and we went downstairs.

It was a beautiful day, warmer than any I'd seen in Salisbury so far, and we talked about my sisters and the house and the The Beard's allergy to Larry's dog hairs — and somehow we found our way back to the Cathedral Close.

"Come, let's go into the cathedral," Mum said. "The last time I was here was with your father."

The cloisters were nearly deserted, and even the cathedral was empty. We walked down the central aisle, until my mother suddenly stopped in front of Longspee's tomb.

"Your father loved this tomb," she said. "He knew

everything about this knight. I can't even remember his name. . . ."

"Longspee," I said. "William Longspee."

"Exactly! That was it. They really teach you a lot of things in this school! Your father was obsessed with him. He once took me up to Old Sarum, just to show me the spot where Longspee died. Did you know they say he was poisoned?"

"Yes," I said. "And he loved his wife very much."

"Really?"

"Mum?" I asked back. "Did Dad ever tell you whether he met Longspee?"

"*Met?* What do you mean?"

She looked completely puzzled. So, he hadn't. Or he'd just never told her. Just like me.

"Do you believe in ghosts, Mum?"

She looked at Longspee's marble face and then let her glance run over all the other dead who were sleeping between the columns.

"No," she finally said. "No, I don't. If there were such

a thing as ghosts, then I think your father would've visited me after he died." She reached into her bag. "Oh, why did I return that horrid handkerchief to that lady?" she muttered, her voice already muffled by tears. "I should have known I'd need it again!"

I took her hand. "It's good that he didn't come back, Mum," I said quietly. "Because it means that he's happy wherever he is now. Ghosts are not very happy, you know?"

She looked at me as if she were seeing me for the first time. "Since when do you think about ghosts, Jon? Everybody is suddenly talking about ghosts. Did Matthew put that nonsense in your head?"

"No!" I answered. "We've just been talking about it at school." It didn't feel right to lie in the cathedral, but I think on that day my mother was in no shape to hear the whole Longspee-Stourton story. The Beard and I only told her many years later, and I'm still not sure she believed us.

"At school?" Mum asked incredulously. "They talk about ghosts there? What subject is this?"

"Oh, um, English?" I sputtered. "You know, Shakespeare and all that."

"Ah, yes," she said. "Sure." Then she squeezed my hand and ruffled my hair (extremely embarrassing for an eleven-year-old). "What do you think? Shall we say good-bye to the dead knight and find ourselves some dinner?"

"Good idea," I mumbled. For a moment I thought I could see Longspee between the columns, with a smile on his face. It was a few weeks after that when I asked the knight whether he remembered meeting another boy named Whitcroft approximately thirty-five years earlier. But my father had never called Longspee, because even back then my dad had been simply a happy person and hadn't needed any help.

"What about friends?" my mother asked as we walked side by side across the grass in front of the cathedral. "Those boys we met by the school—are they your best friends?"

"Angus and Stu?" I asked. "Yes. Although...no, not really."

"And what's that supposed to mean, now?" Mum asked.

The evening sun shone on the old houses around us, and I realized we were standing in the exact spot where Stourton had caught up with me and where Bonapart had picked me up from the ground.

"My best friend is a girl," I said. "And you know her uncle. In fact, you're going to marry him."

A Note From the Author

I first had the idea for this book many years ago when, on my way to visit my English publisher, Barry Cunningham, my family and I stopped for a few days in Salisbury.

When I stepped into the cathedral, I immediately knew I'd come to the kind of place that is unforgettable and that immediately tells you many stories. We took a tour with a German guide, and I heard about William Longspee for the first time. And the seed was sown.

I returned later to visit the Salisbury Cathedral School, for I knew that the boy who was going to be the hero of my story went to school there. I spoke with the students about their ghost stories, and they gave me a tour of the school and their favorite places. I learned about the "island," and I saw the painting of the chorister whose ghost we meet in the school chapel. The students' helpfulness was unbelievable, and I very much hope that the teachers and pupils of the Cathedral School won't be upset that I took some liberties with my story. Their daily school life is definitely very different from the way I describe it here. I don't think students keep sneaking off, as Jon has to at some point, and there is no Bonapart, only very nice teachers like Peter Smith, who helped me in every possible way.

Of course, I also visited the boardinghouse. No Popplewells

there—they are my invention. There are also no ghosts standing under the windows. But should you ever visit Salisbury, I hope you'll still find a lot of the things I've described.

Even the dean of the cathedral—the only woman in Britain who runs a medieval cathedral—was always ready to help, and I had the privilege of witnessing her admirable work when I attended an evensong and Easter service with my children.

I encountered the same friendliness and helpfulness in Kilmington and Lacock Abbey. I climbed the tower in which William Hartgill found refuge from Lord Stourton. I saw the cellar where the Hartgills were probably kept prisoners, and I followed Ela to Lacock Abbey.

A few words about the other Ella, who helps Jon call Longspee: After my British publisher read the manuscript for this book the first time, he called me and asked how I had come up with that wonderful girl character. I answered, "I stole her!" For Ella Littlejohn is actually Ella Wigram, the eldest daughter of Lionel Wigram, with whom I worked on the book *Reckless* for many years. When I found out that William Longspee had a very famous wife by the name of Ela, I thought: "Hold on, Cornelia! Why don't you put a girl named Ella in the story, who reminds the knight of his wife?" It was, of course, a perfect coincidence that Lionel's daughter was also called Ella, and I couldn't have wished for a better inspiration for my character.

Ella has read several versions of this story, and of course I asked for her permission before I put her into the book.

And there is another real-life inspiration for a character in this story: Wellington, the dog who distracts the guards at Stonehenge. He is based on the faithful dog companion of my friend Elinor Bagenal, and he was also asked for his permission before he was turned into a character.

And one final point: There really are ghost tours in Salisbury! How else would I have come up with the idea that that's what Ella's grandmother does?

So... this is my most heartfelt THANK YOU to all the lovely people in Salisbury, Kilmington, and Lacock who helped me with the story. My special thanks go to Peter Smith, Tim Tatten Brown, and June Osborne, the dean of the cathedral. I also want to thank Elinor for all the research and for introducing me to the real Wellington. Thank you again to Ella, for being such a great model for my character. And as far as Jon is concerned, my American editor told me he reminds her of a youthful version of my British agent, Andrew Nurnberg. That was not intentional, but the more I think about it... yes, there are some obvious similarities!

Warmest greetings from Los Angeles,
Cornelia

Glossary

An **abbey** is a special kind of monastery, or home to a religious community of monks or nuns. A monastery may be elevated to an abbey if, for example, a certain number of monks or nuns live there together for a period of time. The leader of an abbey is called an abbot or abbess.

The **Battle of Bouvines** took place on July 27, 1214, near the village of Bouvines in France. The battle, fought between the French king Philip II and an English-German army led by the German king and Holy Roman Emperor Otto IV, ended in a French victory. The battle greatly influenced the development of France, England, and the Holy Roman Empire.

Richard Beauchamp lived in England in the fifteenth century. He became bishop of Salisbury in 1450. He died in 1481 and was buried in Salisbury.

Hubert de Burgh was born around 1165. He was the Earl of Kent and prime minister of England and Ireland. He was one of the most influential English nobles of his time. He died on May 12, 1243.

John Cheney was born around 1447. He was a squire, stable master, and captain of the king's bodyguard under Edward IV, king of England. He married the widow of William, Baron Stourton, and took the title Lord Stourton of Stourton. After Richard III became king of England, Sir John sided with Henry Tudor and joined the revolt against the king. In 1486, he was made a Knight of the Garter, the highest order of knighthood. After Henry Tudor became king (Henry VII), Sir John was raised in rank, becoming Lord Cheney of Falstone Cheney. He sat in Parliament and was speaker of the House of Commons. He died around 1499. His effigy can be seen in Salisbury Cathedral.

A **cloister** is a courtyard in a monastery or cathedral. The central open area is surrounded by covered passages. Cloisters were important places for religious activities and for teaching; they were also used as gardens and graveyards.

A **Crusade** was one of several wars of Christians against Muslims in the Holy Land, an area making up the modern nations of Israel and Jordan in the region now called the Middle East. Historians usually describe seven separate Crusades that took place between 1096 and 1270. These conflicts were fought mainly for religious and economic reasons. After the First Crusade, the term *Crusade* was often extended to describe wars against other non-Christian people and even against the Orthodox Christian churches of the East.

A **crusader** is someone who took part in a Crusade. Most of the crusaders were monks, knights, or noblemen, but large numbers of the rural population also joined the Crusades. Even convicted criminals followed the call, probably to escape punishment or in the hope of finding loot in the East.

Druids were the spiritual leaders of societies of tribal peoples called Celts. According to ancient writings, the druids also advised and healed, looked into the future, and performed rituals and sacrifices.

Eleanor of Aquitaine was born in 1122 in Poitiers in France. She was married to the French king Louis VII. When their marriage was annulled after fifteen years, Eleanor married again. Her second husband was King Henry II of England. Eleanor of Aquitaine made history as queen of two countries and as mother to two kings, Richard I and John of England. As one of the most influential women of the Middle Ages, she supported poets, musicians, and painters. She died on April 1, 1204, at the monastery of Fontevrault in France.

Hamlet is the prince of Denmark and the title character in a play by the English writer William Shakespeare. The ghost of Hamlet's father appears and reveals that his brother Claudius murdered him. Hamlet spends the rest of the play seeking revenge against his uncle.

William Hartgill lived in Kilmington in the English county of Wiltshire. From 1543, Hartgill worked as the manager of an estate owned by the Stourtons, a noble family. Hartgill argued with Charles Stourton, who locked him in the church tower at Kilmington and robbed him of his possessions. After Hartgill appealed to the courts, Lord Stourton had him, his men, and his son John Hartgill killed and hastily buried.

Henry II was born on March 5, 1133, in Le Mans in France. In 1154, he was crowned "king of England." He was the first to use that title instead of "king of the English." He was also known as Henry Curtmantel ("short robe") because he always wore a short cloak. He died on July 6, 1189, in Chinon, France.

Henry VII was born on January 28, 1457, in Wales. At that time, two royal families, the Tudors and the Yorks, were fighting the Wars of the Roses for the English crown. Henry, a Tudor, fled to Brittany in France. He returned with a strong army and beat Richard III, of the Yorks, in the Battle of Bosworth Field in 1485. From then until his death on April 21, 1509, Henry VII was king of England. He is considered the founder of the Tudor dynasty (a group or family that stays in power a long time).

Henry VIII was born on June 28, 1491, in Greenwich, England. He became king of England after the death of Henry VII, his father. Henry VIII was married six times, which led to a break with the Catholic Church. He founded the Church of England and made himself its head. Henry VIII died on January 28, 1547, in London.

An **illegitimate** child was born to parents who were not married to each other. The term *bastard* was used in the Middle Ages to refer to such children. When a nobleman had a child with a woman of a lower social rank, that child could inherit the father's rank only if his lawful wife could not have children of her own and there were no other eligible relatives.

James II was born on October 14, 1633, in London and was crowned king of England on April 23, 1685. As a Catholic, he was accused by Protestant rivals of trying to lead the kingdom back to the Catholic faith and to establish absolute power for himself. He was overthrown during the Glorious Revolution in

1689. His daughter Mary II took the throne with her husband, William of Orange, who ruled as William III. James died on September 16, 1701, in Saint-Germain-en-Laye, France.

John Lackland was born on December 24, 1167, in Oxford, England. The youngest son of King Henry II, he was called Lackland because his father gave him very little land. John became king of England in 1199, and his troubled reign led to the drafting of the Magna Carta and inspired the Robin Hood legends. He died on October 19, 1216, in Nottinghamshire in England.

Lacock Abbey was founded by Ela Longspee in 1229 in the village of Lacock in England. After the death of her husband, William Longspee, Ela joined the monastery as a nun in 1238, and in 1241 she became its first abbess.

Ela Longspee was born in Amesbury, England. Her exact date of birth is unknown. When she was a child, Ela was kidnapped by her own mother and taken to France. There she was rescued by a knight disguised as a troubadour, whom Richard the Lionheart had sent to find her. She was the Countess of Salisbury and married William Longspee in 1197 or 1198. After William's death, Ela founded Lacock Abbey. When she died in 1261, she was buried at the abbey.

William Longspee, born between 1175 and 1180, was an illegitimate son of the English king Henry II. He was called Longspee because his favored weapon was the long sword, also known as the longspée. On the orders of his brother King Richard I, he married Ela, Countess of Salisbury, and became the Earl of Salisbury. In 1220, William was present at the laying of the foundation stone of Salisbury Cathedral. He died on March 7, 1226, and was the first to be buried in the new cathedral.

Angus MacNisse was the first bishop of Connor in Ireland. He is thought to be the founder of the Abbey of Kells. His date of birth is unknown. He probably died in 514.

Magna Carta means "Great Charter." Signed on June 15, 1215, the Magna Carta was an agreement between King John of England and the nobility who opposed him. It set out certain basic rights of the nobility and promised that the church would be free from control by the king. Today, four of the original handwritten copies of the Magna Carta survive. The best-preserved one is kept in the library of Salisbury Cathedral.

Napoléon Bonaparte was born on August 15, 1769, in Corsica, a French island in the Mediterranean Sea. After serving in the French military, he organized an overthrow of the government in 1799. Napoléon became the first consul (a high official) of the French Republic before crowning himself emperor of France in 1804. He fought and won many wars. After a defeat in Russia, he was exiled, or sent away from his home country. He later escaped and returned to France but was finally beaten at the Battle of Waterloo in Belgium in 1815. He died in exile on the South Atlantic island of Saint Helena on May 5, 1821.

Old Sarum is the oldest settlement in Salisbury. It was probably inhabited as early as 3000 BC. The first settlement was on a hill to the north of Salisbury's present-day location.

Richard I was born on September 8, 1157, in Oxford. In 1189, he forced his father, King Henry II, to give up the throne to him. He was known as Richard the Lionheart, and many legends describe him as a wise and good king. But tales of Richard as a hero have little to do with reality. He liked to present himself as the ideal knight, and his military deeds were hugely exaggerated. Richard I died on April 6, 1199, in Châlus in France.

Robin Hood is an English folk hero. The oldest documents that mention Robin Hood describe him as a dangerous robber who attacked noblemen and priests. In later writings, he is described in more positive terms: as a nobleman who took from the rich and gave to the poor. According to legend, Robin and his men hid in Sherwood Forest and Barnsdale Forest. Stories of the outlaw Robin Hood remain popular, but most experts say there is no evidence that he actually existed.

Rugby is a sport that started in England. Two teams of thirteen to fifteen players compete with an oval ball. Each team tries to place the ball behind the line of the opposing team. The ball cannot be thrown forward and can only be kicked or carried.

Salisbury Cathedral School was founded in 1091 by Bishop Osmund in Old Sarum. One hundred fifty years later, it was moved to Salisbury. Since 1947 the school has been housed in the Bishop's Palace on the grounds of the cathedral.

A **sarcophagus** is a stone coffin. In the Middle Ages, kings, noblemen, and high-ranking officials of the church were buried in sarcophagi, which can be seen in many churches and cathedrals throughout Europe.

A **squire** was a young man who was trained by a knight in the use of weapons.

The name **Stonehenge** is Old English for "hanging stones." Stonehenge began as a burial site in the late Stone Age. Centuries later, circles of massive upright stones were placed at the site. Several large circles are arranged around one another, all centered on the same point. Legends surrounding Stonehenge are as old as the structure itself. One myth says the wizard Merlin used magic to bring the stones from Ireland.

Charles Stourton was born in 1521 in the county of Wiltshire in England. Lord Stourton and four of his servants killed William Hartgill and his son John. For this murder, Stourton was sentenced to death and executed on March 6, 1556, in the marketplace at Salisbury. Stourton was hanged but not beheaded, as would have been his right according to his social rank. He was buried in Salisbury Cathedral.

The **Duke of Wellington** is a hereditary English title. The title was first given in 1814 to Arthur Wellesley, the military leader who defeated Napoléon Bonaparte at the Battle of Waterloo the following year. Later, Wellington was twice elected prime minister of England.

William of Orange was born on November 14, 1650, in Den Haag in the Netherlands. From 1672 he was the governor of the Netherlands. After the Glorious Revolution, when King James II was overthrown, William and his wife became king and queen of England, ruling as William III and Mary II. William died on March 19, 1702, in Kensington in England.